LOS ANGELES

ALSO BY RICH IVES

POETRY
Notes from the Water Journals

Light from a Small Brown Bird
(expanded edition of *Notes from the Water Journals*)

PROSE
Sharpen (chapbook)
Tunneling to the Moon

EDITOR
Rain in the Forest, Light in the Trees (Northwest Poetry Anthology)
From Timberline to Tidepool (Northwest Fiction Anthology)
The Truth About the Territory (Northwest Nonfiction Anthology)
Evidence of Fire (German Poetry in Translation Anthology)

TRANSLATOR
Yesterday I Was Leaving (poetry—Johannes Bobrowski)

TEXT
A Dirty Little Book About Writing the Truth

THE BALLOON CONTAINING THE WATER CONTAINING THE NARRATIVE BEGINS LEAKING

STORIES BY

RICH IVES

LOS ANGELES

Copyright © 2015 by Rich Ives. All rights reserved. Published in the United States by What Books Press, the imprint of the Glass Table Collective, Los Angeles.

Publisher's Cataloging-In-Publication Data

Ives, Rich, 1951-

  The balloon containing the water containing the narrative begins leaking : stories / by Rich Ives.

    pages ; cm

  ISBN: 978-0-9962276-0-5

  1. Surrealism--Fiction. 2. Short stories, American. I. Title.

PS3559.V45 B35 2015

813/.54

Cover art: Gronk, *untitled*, watercolor and ink, 2015
Book design by Ash Goodwin, AshGood.com

What Books Press
363 South Topanga Canyon Boulevard
Topanga, CA 90290

WHATBOOKSPRESS.COM

THE BALLOON
CONTAINING THE
WATER CONTAINING
THE NARRATIVE
BEGINS LEAKING

CONTENTS

A BRIEF HISTORY OF LOVE
AND DEATH IN THE BLACK FOREST

PIEMAN'S SOLILOQUY: "It is said of me that I do not like to talk much. That is not quite true. I speak very slowly. I come from the Black Forest. I have rings in my nose and I am very strong. It is said of me that I can lift three oxen by raising my strong nose in the air. That is not quite true, either."

In the Black Forest there are many trees. That is the first thing one must know about the Black Forest.

Pieman is dying. Charlotte is a dream, a dream that lives within Pieman's dream. Imagine her standing on a ledge at the mouth of a cave, stretching, skin rippling over waking muscles, buttocks tensing, torso shifting the ripples the way lakewater moves sand along its edges.

Pieman wears a hat in his dream. Pieman's hat has nothing about it to suggest that, removed, it would reveal anything in the way of grandeur. At best it might suggest more of the gray and white streaks of tangled hair dangling like moss from the sides of his head. This would be an illusion. The hat hides his bald spot.

Pieman's suit in the dream is a gray sag interrupted by a black vest with a gold watch-chain dangling from the left pocket. His shoes are black wingtips.

Once a long time ago a Chinese emperor came to the Black Forest. He had
a wise man with him and three barrels of gold carp. They were looking for
a place to grow snow peas. If the gold carp came back in two days from the
bottom of the lake, this would be the place where the snow peas could grow
and be brought to soak in the lake water and be cooked in ways that would
make them more exciting to the emperor's palate than anything he had ever
tasted. The wise man assured the emperor that this would be the place. He
dumped the gold carp into the Black Lake. That is how the Bay of Bones got
its name.

Imagine Charlotte in a cave, crouched near the fire, thoughts flickering like
the play of light and shadow as the fire warms her. She imagines moss in the
forest. She reaches to touch it and a few feet away a salamander darts under a
rock. She sits in a tree in the darkness, metamorphic, her owl head swiveling
quietly, gazing. A flash of light sparkles from the broken surface of a mirror-
calm lake. A loon surfaces with a fish in its beak.
Charlotte frisks with her puppies. She watches the fire.

In the Black Forest there is sometimes black rain. That is the second thing
one must know about the Black Forest.

Some nights Pieman lies in bed and pretends he is not from the Black
Forest. Taitum, the Black Gypsy, comes to take him to Marlaine, the sultry
one, his lover and secret eye. They go off together on wild adventures and
forget that they are not meant to be so carefree.

From the ledge at the mouth of the cave, Charlotte can see, on those few
days when it is not raining or cloudy, nearly all of the forest, glimpses of most
of the lakes scattered among the birch, beech, willow and oak, and the fading
roll of hills flattening into the distance, barely visible beyond the thinning of
the trees collected in the small valley like green water in a calm inlet.

One night a woman with a gold ankle-chain and beady eyes came to Pieman
in a dream. She pushed at him and he rolled a little, but he didn't move any more
after that. He woke up in a cold sweat and scared himself when he saw the pale
face and the frightened expression in the mirror he had mounted in the ceiling.

In the Black Lake there are reflections of all the people who have ever lived in the Black Forest. That is a thing one must know about the Black Lake.

Pieman counted the rabbits till his eyes blurred and he started to get dizzy. They moved about almost sluggishly, but with an energy lurking beneath the sluggishness, like children just waking up.

Three young boys ran up the path carrying burlap bags full of cherries, throwing them at each other. They spotted the rabbits and showered them with cherries. When the rabbits weren't frightened off by the first attack, the boys chased them into the forest.

Pieman laughed and headed for the stream. A burlap bag was lying by a small patch of tall grass. He took a drink from the stream and sat down in the grass. He was barely awake when he heard more children's voices, but the heat carried him into sleep.

And so now I must tell you how it goes.

She said hello. He said hello. They talked. Mostly about nothing. He kissed. She kissed. After a while they made love. First he made love, and then later on she made love. They stayed together. And then they didn't stay together. And then they did. And then they did some more things together, but they didn't like it so much.

Hello, you have a nice smile.

Okay, but you have to be gentle.

Still, it was no good pretending like that. It was silly. No, it was boring. Anyway they stayed together.

Neither one of them told the other about the other.

Pieman imagined two children. He imagined he was one of them. He was asking a young girl did she want to go swimming, and he was smiling when she said she didn't bring her swimsuit. And then he was splashing and beckoning to the young girl. Don't be afraid. No one will see us.

Someone was laughing. It sounded familiar and for a moment Pieman thought he was the one who was laughing. But it was someone else, and it was getting louder.

Slowly, Pieman opened his eyes. Cherry juice dripped from his hat, and the rich dark stains were soaking into his clothing. Pieman laughed. A bearded man in overalls sputtered something about the children. His beard quivered when he laughed, and his bald head sparkled in the sunlight.

Charlotte begins working her way down to the forest. Her movements are cautious, deer-like. Suddenly she disappears. The motionless contours of her body blend in with the shapes and colors of the rocks and clay along the path.

Now I have to tell you about the black rain. Everyone in the Black Forest knows about the black rain. If it were not for the black rain, there would be no Black Lake and all of the black trees in the Black Forest would die. If it were not for the black rain, there would be no love in the Black Forest. Sometimes the lovers in the Black Forest go for days without rain, but that is not a thing that is very pleasant. Love in the Black Forest is warm and dark and moist and always a little different and a little deeper than anyone ever thought it would be. That too, is because of the black rain.

Small fern-like plants jut out into the narrowing pathway. The dew, which still lingers on them, makes them cold to the touch. Occasionally Charlotte shivers as she brushes against them. As she reaches a clearing or when a few rays of sunlight break through the trees, the dew from these plants makes her skin glisten.

The small sack of pecans in the inside coat pocket of Pieman's cherry-stained gray suit tore open, and a couple of pecans fell out. Pieman put the torn sack and the rest of the pecans in his half-filled bag of cherries. Something moved at the end of the meadow. Pieman followed the path to a stream. Nearby was a patch of rhubarb. He began stuffing the rhubarb in the burlap bag.

Charlotte bends to drink from a small lake, tensed, wary. Suddenly she loses her footing on the moss-covered rocks and plunges noisily into the lake. After the first startled glances along the deserted shore, she laughs and swims to a clump of willows, half swallowed by the lake. She tears off a small branch, puts it in her mouth, and swims back across the lake.

Pieman's soliloquy: "Sometimes I wonder what it was like before there was a Black Forest. This is not a thing that is very pleasant to think about, and I wonder if something isn't wrong with me to think about it like that.

I am a very strong man, and even here where people come in so many strange shapes, I am bigger and stronger than most.

But I don't feel very strong when I think about this thing, and I wonder if I am not so very smart to be thinking about this thing. Maybe it should be that I do what I am going to do, and that is that. Yes, I think that is a good way. I should be like that."

Pieman cupped his hands and dipped them in the stream. A few drops of sweat fell from his forehead. As he drank he noticed a broken bone stuck in the mud. He picked it up and began making marks. He erased the marks with his foot and began again. He erased the marks again, his gestures less casual. With the blunt end of the bone, he drew a circle. With the pointed, broken end he began drawing delicate thin lines radiating out from the circle. Where the circle was less round, he drew a straight line, as if this were a floor for the figure to rest upon.

The sun was sinking beneath the horizon.

Charlotte is digging roots near the lake. She pauses to rest and noticing the texture of the lichen on a nearby rock, touches it lightly with her fingers. Then she goes back to her digging. Soon she has enough roots. For a few quiet moments she watches the lake, then she disappears into the forest.

Walking along a widening path, Pieman came to a meadow. He set his bag in the grass and lay down. He dreamed there was a peacock in the meadow. He watched it for a long time. He dreamed there was a young woman lying naked in the grass, limbs spread as if to make an angel in snow.

Charlotte begins climbing the path to the cave. In one hand she carries the roots she dug near the lake, in the other she carries an assortment of plants, red berries still clinging to them. In her mouth she carries the willow branch just as she did swimming across the lake.

Pieman imagines the sun going down. Suddenly it is very cold. Pieman imagines a cave high up on a hillside.

He builds a fire in the cave.

Charlotte sits by the fire, chewing on the end of a willow branch. She draws it between her lips, looks at it, and chews on it some more. Slowly, the fibers form a soft point. Then she begins grinding the plants and roots and berries in a clay bowl with a stone. When enough juices have collected in the bowl, she throws the remaining hard fibers in the fire and goes to a place farther back in the cave, directed by the sound of dripping water, to where the floor is a wet clay. She adds some of this clay to the mixture in the bowl and returns to the fire.

Pieman climbing a hillside. An old man, tired, out of breath, sweating, stumbling . . .

A meadow in the valley, a bearded man in overalls breaking into hearty laughter, a cherry pie steaming in the center of the meadow.

The hallway of an old apartment building. A door opens, and an elderly woman wearing a pheasant-feather hat steps out into the morning. She smiles when she sees the pecan pie steaming in the cold hallway.

Imagine bending over a stream to take a drink and finding a fresh rhubarb pie beside you.

Pieman enters the cave and leans back against the wall. As the sun goes down, it lights one wall of the cave where there is a painting of the sun going down.

In the Black Forest death is liquid. Rain is an animal. Dreams become reality so quickly sleep can be exhausting.

Charlotte pulls the pie from the oven. Whistling, she sets the pie on an open window ledge. It begins raining.

A WARM RAIN BEGAN TO FALL

IT WASN'T JUST being stood up that bothered him, he told himself.
It was that he had begun to care about her. That little tick in his throat
sometimes when he wanted to say something nice to her, and the way he
seemed to be nervous too much, an odd sort of nervousness because physically
he felt very comfortable with her.

For days after it happened he turned in on himself and had waxing dreams
where he was driving a small car on a lonely country road during a storm. The
animals in the fields seemed agitated; even the sullen cows didn't seem so sullen. The
wheat rolled about in constantly shifting waves that kept drawing his attention back
away from the road. But that was all. He never had the accident he was expecting.

Two weeks later he had the same dream again, but this time he came to an
out-of-the-way roadhouse, an old one with a gas pump and an old- fashioned cafe
with a long wooden porch on the front and a barn off to the side. A metal sign
so worn the name of the cafe wasn't clear enough to read anymore was banging
in the wind. He stopped the car and got out, stood there with his hair huffing in
the wind, staring off towards the barn where a woman stood, facing him. She was
too far away for him to see her face, but she waited patiently while he watched,
the storm between them. Finally he grew calm, and a warm rain began to fall. It
seemed as if he could feel each individual drop as once more he began the long
walk back to himself.

TRAIN SONG

THE MAN WAS SHORT. He wore a heavy overcoat and a round black hat much like an English bowler but less conspicuous. A fresh snow covered the street, and passing cars made a soft crunching sound. He stood by the door to the cafe with no apparent purpose, neat, clean-shaven, and holding himself severely in check, except for the forlorn expression on his face.

He was a painter, though the only current evidence of that in his tiny studio apartment was a disorderly clump of brushes, paints and unused canvas piled in the corner near the dusty window. A single portrait, unframed, hung from the wall above the unmade bed. The colors were bright, almost harsh, but somehow toned down by the somber expression of the half-naked woman drawn with minimal lines, her olive shoulders diving away from her neck, her chin raised and climbing, one eye peering suspiciously through the veil of a large black hat, the other covered by its brim.

A young woman in an old fur coat, her hair in braids, approached the man from the broken, cobbled street. They stood next to each other for a moment, not speaking, and turned to enter the café. At a booth in the back, Pietre and Sarah sat quietly, slowly unwrapping themselves from their winter clothing.

Sarah took a breath and held it. She grasped her braids in each hand as if gathering force to say something that badly needed saying. But that was as far as she got.

Mittenz spotted them at their booth the moment he entered the door, a small cloud of snow trailing into the cafe behind him like an abused and needy pet. Mittenz was a druggist and an amateur art dealer with a few unexpectedly large sales to his credit, a short fat balding man with altogether too much energy for such a dismal day.

His wire rim glasses had a habit of sliding down his nose until he raised a stubby finger to push them back up again, a gesture he used to punctuate his conversation and a trait that had somehow become endearing to Sarah, if not to her sullen painter. Mittenz could have been trusted had he not fancied himself a brilliantly perceptive art critic and taken to pontificating on the excesses and deficiencies of Pietre's most recent efforts.

A gray pall descended on the table with Mittenz, melting a moment of pleasant surprise into an old and stubborn clog of restraint. He settled, sagging on his chair and not even the bright reflections from the fresh snow swirling at the café's many windows could stir the stagnant acceptance of habitual coagulant intimacies.

Dinner at Sarah's was less gloomy, but Pietre's current failure to paint anything he liked was edging into its ninth month, and he felt it consuming him, eating away at his future.

He spoke of it to Sarah, as he had on numerous previous occasions, and some obvious comment she made in a voice like Mittenz's about producing art being like giving birth made them both laugh and try to remember if they had made love nine months ago. They decided they had, drank an extra bottle of Chianti to celebrate, and after discussing how inappropriate it was to compare an artist to a pregnant woman, went to bed.

Pietre woke in the middle of the night, left Sarah an ambiguous intimate note of gratitude and went home. He was afraid if he stayed he would spoil the temporary relief of the night by letting daylight again defeat him.

Snow in the mountains. Chickens. An old German woman with a large brown satchel dozing on a bench in the depot. A Belgian soldier snuffles up his last piece of chocolate.

The train is coming.

He woke late again, knowing he had been dreaming, but was unable to remember the dream. He poured cold water in the ceramic basin and splashed it on his face, running his wet fingers back over his hair. He wiped his hands on the old pair of pajama bottoms he had worn to bed for the first time since he had come to the city. A quick pulse of freedom flashed over him, as in a dream he had forgotten but still felt, the same pulse, he remembered, which had arrived without explanation the first night alone in this room when he had buried the pajamas in the bottom drawer of the old oak dresser and slept naked with the window open.

By evening the painting was nearly finished. The ice man, whose cry annoyed him well before dawn each morning, was there on the street with his cart. So were two ladies of the evening, who were usually farther up the street, standing under brightly colored parasols with their backs slightly arched for the benefit of any interested gentleman who might happen by. The square brick building behind them with some unknown official purpose stood securely on the corner. He didn't recognize it, but it felt familiar.

He stood back from the easel and admired the angles of the new railroad trestle, the way it passed through this first quiet painting, and he imagined the sound as the evening express rattled by outside the window and the small apartment began to shake.

For a week the paintings came quickly. On Monday it was the young girl by the fountain, palm trees towering over her as she leaned against the railing, one arm self-consciously adjusting a stray strand of hair. Tuesday it was the two boys in tight pants, who were forever waiting at their table in the blue-light bar. Wednesday was for final touches and a trip to the market for more paints. Thursday a piano player sat on the canvas with his hands outstretched, and Friday the keys began to appear beneath his fingers. By Sunday that painting too was complete.

Sunday evening Pietre went to the bar to hear the musicians that gathered there each week. Sarah showed up an hour or so after he did, and the glances they exchanged were a comfort to him against his renewed fears. Then Mittenz came in the door and sat down at their table.

"How's the Bohemian crowd?"

"Free and careless." Sarah threw the expression into the air like a broken toy.

"How are you, Pietre?" Mittenz addressed Pietre directly with an appearance of genuine good will, and it crossed Pietre's mind that perhaps

Mittenz was making a gesture of apology for his manner the last time they met. Suddenly he was not in the mood for conversation, and he rose from the table, flinging his scarf back over his shoulder like a gesture of defiance.

"I'm painting." Pietre touched Sarah on the shoulder with a light squeeze and handed the empty salt-shaker to the waiter. The annoyance pleased him.

Waves folding against a rowboat, slapping against the soft wood of an old dock like a woman's hands on bread dough.

Two children running up the path from the lake, waving their arms frantically. The train is coming.

Pietre leaned the paintings against the wall and sat down across the room with a cup of peppermint tea. He was afraid to question his good luck, but he knew he had to understand what had happened in order to be able to continue without another dry spell. Soon he was sleeping, teacup still perched between the palms of both hands. He woke from a pleasant dream of sledding on his parents' farm in Minnesota, and he began to see objects in the paintings across the room that were linked to his past--the cut of a hat, the color and style of a coat button, the particular shade and pattern of the sky behind a figure . . . Something in each of the paintings now seemed clearly part of his youth, and he decided to concentrate on that.

He got little sleep during the following week, and the two paintings he brought to near completion still felt to him as if they were missing something. He woke from his sleep on Sunday night feeling as if he had dreamt a revelation. Nervous, he tried to remember the dream. He could find no pattern in the stray images he could recall. In fact everything in the dream seemed to be wrong. His paintings appeared in the dream in styles he had never used, never admired, but in each one there was the expected familiar object--not the ones he had used, but new ones with familiar feelings attached but no memory of the item's place in his past--a cracked teacup with a pattern he recognized, a blue rocking horse with a cracked left ear, a plaid flannel shirt with a familiar stain . . . He wanted his life back. He wanted the past to forget him. He decided he needed a signature, an object, from his present life, just as the first paintings after his block had needed something from his past.

He went back to sleep feeling confident he would continue painting indefinitely, and in the morning he charted out relationships between the objects in his apartment to give a pattern, a structure, to how they might appear in his next paintings. With that done, he felt a need to see Sarah and explain to her how things had changed. He would compare it to movies for her (she was addicted to them). He would explain how his "objects" appearing in his paintings were like Alfred Hitchcock's cameo appearances. Not important to the plot or the film as a whole but important to the director, to him a cosmic joke, a thread of visual coherence, a signature, an intrusion of present reality into the imagination's structured artifice.

But Sarah was not at her apartment. Nor was she in any of the places where he looked for her.

Back at his apartment Pietre was struck by the clutter and confusion he had allowed to engulf his living space. He began immediately to put things in order, and he found that as he cleaned and sorted he was putting each item associated with Sarah into a neat little nest in the corner of the room. He went to the window and stared, willing her appearance, a half-framed figure emerging from the continuing welcome anonymity of snowfall.

But the woman was not Sarah, and her torn parasol depressed Pietre.

An old man patting the earth around a tulip, shading his eyes from sunlight reflected off an irrigation ditch. A skinny woman drinking lemonade on the porch. A child building roads in the garden with handfulls of sand and a broken rolling pin. The train is coming.

The following day Pietre ran into Sarah at the supermarket and suddenly felt very happy, energetic. He offered to cook supper for her, and they returned to his apartment. He noticed that she seemed to appreciate the new, organized cleanliness. She sat in the chair in the corner of the apartment where he had placed the objects he associated with her, and he thought of the objects there one by one with a little bubble of emotion surrounding each of them as he cooked supper. It seemed a little odd to be doing this, but it gave him an idea for another painting, and he grew even more pleased with himself.

The dinner was nothing fancy, spaghetti with broccoli in a cheese sauce, but it was tasty enough, and a bottle of Chardonnay improved their mood.

In bed they shared a renewed enthusiasm for sex and for each other, and they awoke twice during the night to return to their lovemaking. Pietre had a dream about the nest of bubbles he had made in the living room. He caressed

Sarah's stomach and curled his body around her, squeezing gently.

He placed his mouth against her and imagined he was forming another bubble in which to receive some part of their future. He did it again and again. He released each one slowly, imagined them floating off to the nest in the living room. An odd but somehow comforting dream, Pietre did not try to tell it to Sarah. She snuggled up to Pietre with a little giggle and finally a contented sigh.

Something was finished and Pietre felt good about it. He was not sure exactly what it was, but it felt right. Maybe his new paintings had taken him to a new stage, and it was time to cash in on them and begin something else. Maybe it was Sarah. Things felt right again with Sarah, and he caught himself thinking from time to time of leaving the city with her. Where they might go was all quite vague, but there was something exciting about it.

As with many such hopeful prospects, the hitch, however, was money. Pietre realized he would have to prevail upon Mittenz to use his connections to help get his paintings into a gallery. And that, of course, required Mittenz's approval of Pietre's new work. He left messages at Mittenz's favorite haunts (Mittenz was not a man who could be counted on to live any one place for any reasonable length of time) requesting his presence for dinner three days hence. Sarah would help with the food and provide a useful bridge between the two men. Pietre knew he could count on Sarah for this, but hated asking her. Mittenz had a diplomat's ability for using favors to create advantageous situations, and more than one of Mittenz's mistresses had fallen to him in this manner. It made Pietre nervous. He trusted Sarah, perhaps even more now than before, but he knew too well the truth in one of Mittenz's favorite phrases, which he turned so well to his own purposes—"Everyone gets lonely"—and it was often followed by, "even when they're not alone."

A young girl sips nervously at her tea. The porter hands her a note. The note is written on hotel stationary. A man slips out the dining car door. Outside a dog is herding sheep. A white horse stands on the ridge. A woman carrying a milk pail stops to rest at the top of a small hill. She watches a man and a woman kiss. They each have an orange in their coat pocket. And the train is coming.

At first the dinner conversation turned enthusiastically on Pietre's new paintings, and Mittenz seemed genuinely impressed with what he called

Pietre's "return to the bright palette of the stars," even if he remained
preoccupied. He had even seemed enthusiastic about taking the paintings east
to the larger galleries. Once Pietre's apprehensions over Mittenz's acceptance
of his new work had subsided, he began to feel Mittenz's preoccupation was
Sarah, and the two men exchanged a few sharp remarks over seemingly trivial
matters of taste, which Sarah extended to a humorous imaginary dialogue
between two farmyard roosters. As the night wore on, Mittenz seemed to
take on a distant sadness, and by the time he left, they were all feeling a quiet
finality in their parting.

A blue vase. Flowers. A linen napkin. The steward smiling and nodding.
Lights coming on in houses along the tracks. A woman sips at her peppermint
tea and remembers sitting on the porch all evening. She nibbles on grass and
has conversations with the neighbor's cat. She watches the lights coming on
at dusk and waits for the steady pulse of the insects to help her sleep. Long
after the train has come and gone, she is still sitting on the porch, waiting for
something to help her sleep.

A week after the dinner, Pietre returned to his apartment to find his new
paintings gone. He sat down quietly at the table and stared at the butter knife.
He carefully buttered his hand with the clean knife and stood up, holding it
out in front of him. He laughed and threw the knife at the wall. It didn't stick.
Then he began crying, looking for something to break the windows with. But
even in his anger and frustration he did not think of using his fists. Suddenly
he remembered the key he had given to Mittenz and slumped down in the
chair next to the nest of Sarah objects, and there in front of him, propped in
the crack that ran nearly the full length of the three-legged milking stool Sarah
had given him, was a check for nearly twice the amount he had hoped to get.
He grabbed at the check, and it tore. He pried the bottom half from the crack,
and there was Mittenz's sprawling signature.

Morning and the trees swaying in the wind. A pair of overalls flapping on
a clothesline. A man walking across a plowed field with his dog steps over the
railroad tracks, boots crunching against the coal bedding as he quick steps
to the other side, on his way to the switching station where each morning he
changes the switch on the route the next train will take on its way to Chicago

or Omaha. Then he heads for the barn, where it will take half an hour to get the sluggish tractor to kick in and begin the heavy diesel purr that he greets by calling the dog back from the creek. The dog will ride alongside him on the vibrating metal seat to whichever field needs his attention that day.

A kerosene lamp flickers in the farmhouse window. A woman with her hair in braids begins baking bread as the children wake and get ready to meet the school bus.

Another evening and the children sleeping. The woman turns on the light in the pantry and stares at her husband's unfinished painting. A train engine steams forever across the background of the canvas, a farmer and his dog turning from their work to watch. The foreground is empty, unfinished but for a sky-blue primer and the corner of a brick building disappearing off the edge and into the small shadow of a broken milking stool. The woman steps onto the porch as darkness descends and waits for her husband to return from the fields with his dog, Mittenz, a mongrel that stayed on after a share of the evening's meal one sultry summer night several years ago.

The three of them will rest on the porch as the sun sets and wait for the passage of the night train east. A woman on the train stares out of the club car window at the lights in the farm valley. She begins braiding her hair. A man drinking Chardonnay across the aisle begins humming, "Oh where, oh where can my little dog be?" An art dealer from Chicago, he turns to watch the woman braiding her hair and considers approaching her.

A BRIEF HISTORY OF DIVORCE

I VISIT MY HAT and my hat says, "Somewhere in the little garden of your heart, a boatman sings under a burning moon." I set sail for my shoes and find two tongues preserved in a jar of oil. Now the birds have gathered to feed on a roadkill, and somewhere deep within the raven's throat a cruel young boy rattles a stick against a picket fence, thunderclouds flapping over like rags. My hat sleeps on the porch with the farmer's almanac, dreaming another lecture on the fear of dying.

THE RULES OF ENGAGEMENT

I FOUND UNEXPECTEDLY at my feet a stick of chewing gum. It was an exotic flavor that I no longer remember the name of, tangerine or clove perhaps. I had no intention of chewing it, for it had been thoughtlessly (I could not bring myself to say cleverly) abandoned. Still, it appeared fresh, and I could not convince myself to ignore it. I placed it in the left hand pocket of my coat and carried it for several weeks until it had become mashed and worn and I could no longer read the label. Its fate had once more been altered. It seemed worthless, and I discarded it without a second thought. At least that's what I thought I had done.

It was not the beggar who saw me first but the man in the linen suit, very fashionable yet cool in the raging summer heat. The suited man was asking for donations for an important and fashionable cause, which, I believed, deserved the support he was asking for on its behalf. That was not the reason I gave him three dollar bills. I did it because I wanted to see if he might give one to the ragged man sitting next to him on the sidewalk with a tin cup. I wondered if the two of them were uneasy with each other over sharing this desirable territory where so many people were passing. I did not really expect that the man would give the beggar even one of the dollars, but I wanted to see if I might be wrong. I was not. But the man in the linen suit, who, it now seemed, was a mute, held up a handwritten notice of thanks in front of me, so that I could read it without actually taking it from him. It explained in a few ungrammatical cramped sentences how the donation would support benefits far beyond the immediate cause to which I had donated. I could understand that much without even reading the whole thing. When the man in the linen suit could see that I had tired of deciphering the notice he was holding, he placed it in the beggar's tin cup and quickly walked away.

It's true that I had chosen the blue door because of the woman who had entered during the long, painful and confusing process of selection, which had been placed so deliberately before me. Of the several doors, many, but not all, had been opened and entered by others, both men and women, and I told myself that I was choosing the blue door because of the qualities of character that I had witnessed in the woman's approach, particularly her manner of hesitating as she made her choice. In fact, as I approached, finally, the door of my selection, I did so just as she had, hesitating in the same place and in just the same manner. I did not understand which of the many decisions that lay before me I had just made.

It was a time in which I had been confused by love, alternately ecstatic and miserable and unable to understand how much I was enjoying my misery. I was preparing to take leave of a love, which I did not really believe was over. Nor did I then believe that the events that I imagined might soon be before me could actually cause such an end. I believed only in my own acceptance of the idea of completion as a legitimate cause of change. But I also felt that as long as the acceptance of the events was under my control the events would only appear to take place.

As I made my way towards the most current transient residence of the one I had allowed to ignite my desire, I passed a procession in the streets, which had formed behind a figure held up in the air on a long stick. As I neared the head of the procession and could see the figure clearly, I was shaken to the core with the likeness it bore to my own adored and worriedly thin beloved, raised high now by a man whose exaggeratedly smiling expression appeared to have been painted onto the pillow of his face. I did not know what the procession was for, but I guessed quickly that the figure would be burned, and the followers would celebrate the burning. I knew then that I could no longer meet my love in the manner in which I had planned. I could no longer pursue what I had been seeking. I wandered the streets for many hours until, near morning, I again encountered the procession, returning, it appeared, from the lengthy ceremony, which it had apparently been formed to complete.

And yet the figure on the stick was intact, unburnt, and still smiling its slapstick grin. The followers were subdued, tiredly trudging back to wherever they had come from. One of them seemed to recognize me from earlier and put a hand on my shoulder, yawned and shrugged. "It doesn't do much good to protest, but we do it anyway," he said, and continued tiredly on his way.

There was a time much later when I had been walking, forever it seemed, along a dusty country road and came upon an old friend I had not seen in many years, a friend from my youth with whom I had shared many hopes and dreams though none had been realized before circumstances had taken him from my life. He too had shared his desires for the future with me, and as I struggled to remember them, he sat down on a large stone and gestured for me to sit next to him. He seemed to desire nothing more than that I sit there beside him. He did not speak and did not seem to want to speak. We listened to the wind moving through the rows of corn beside the road as if it were a child unable to resist making the leaves rattle as it passed. The child crossed the road, kicking up a small cloud of dust, and entered the corn on the other side, moving off into the cornfield that seemed to tick and tick again as silence attempted its return and failed. A pheasant crowed in the distance, a sound like a supremely confident rooster, unleashed upon the willing air as if it existed only to carry the noisome rattle and crank. It projected a raw cracked gurgle from the hollow of the bird's chest over the cornfield with a deep rasping climb. After an unexpected pause, to remind us it seemed, of our own presence, a few crickets were tricked into their own greeting of the still absent dusk by a large passing cloud.

My friend stood and brushed the dust from himself just as the now missing child seemed to have done not long before, and he raised his arm in a slow gesture of acceptance that left his hand extended and open, with his palm upwards, as if he were holding something that might choose to fly off if he did not move slowly and carefully. I observed him as carefully as I could and attempted to duplicate the gesture. I did so with great care and concentration, and by the time I had finished, he had turned and was continuing upon his way.

I too agreed that we had been fortunate to have failed in so many foolish dreams and arrived at just a few we could fully appreciate, the ones we might not have noticed if we had been more successful.

I don't understand when it happened, but I remember I was contained in a large room with a group of people laughing and talking in the part of the room that was lit by a number of large candles that offered more light than one would expect from them. The candles were assisted in their hopeless task by two small holes in the ceiling through which the light of the sky outside was descending in aggressive if futile proof of the clarity the sky had to offer if one were not subdued by the equally aggressive heat.

The people were certainly not restrained by anything as familiar as their endlessly repetitious environment, but the close air and clinging warmth of the chamber thrust a torpor like an old musty blanket upon me as I tried to make out what the people were saying. I failed in my task and turned my attention to the candles, which were swaying slowly in the wake of the air disturbed by one of the guests who had left the group to stand alone and observe me. He did not approach, but instead stood as if in meditation and, politely as it is possible to do so, addressed himself to a study of my being. Whatever his study revealed to him, it seemed sufficient, for he shortly returned to the group where he again joined their conversation, which I still could not make out, as if he had not left it and was not returning with anything new to add to it.

It was impossible not to feel a sense of disappointment though I could not discern in myself even an inkling of its source, and I turned my attention to the light dripping down from the holes in the ceiling. The length and contour of the light struck me suddenly, as if two yellow broomsticks had been thrust through the ceiling. I did not want to approach the light, for that would have destroyed the sensation building inside of me that the light was solid, something I could most certainly touch, something I could perhaps break off and strike someone with, so solid did it appear.

The people in the room had stopped talking. The softest of whispers permeated the space between us in a manner I can only describe as the conversation of dust, the same dust I could now see was giving its slowly turning body to the light descending from the two holes in the ceiling, the dust which was now moving in a gently rolling hint at the passage of some larger body. Yet no one had moved.

I imagined various ill-defined qualities of the world outside that I perceived as desirable if only because I did not know enough about them, and I imagined by what means they might use the two holes to enter the room, to enter the room without being conspicuous, not by their own design but through the natural and unpremeditated actions of nature, which I perceived to exist only outside the room.

It had not yet occurred to me to wonder how long I had been in the room.

There was a rasping in my chest when I breathed that reminded me of descriptions I had heard of dying men, but I did not feel like I was dying. I had a fever, but it made me warm and led me easily into dream. I felt as if my nerves had been put on alert, and my body was more awake than when I felt healthy and energetic. Whatever I thought seemed actually to be happening, and I thought of many strange and questionable things, which gave me great pleasure. I even seemed to know as I experienced them that I would not remember what I had experienced.

Several days later, it seemed, I awoke to a great sense of wellbeing and gratitude. I was relaxed and very comfortable, and surprised to find my family gathered around my bed as I opened my eyes. The look in their eyes as I gazed at them, still steeped in my own deep relaxation, brought me quickly to think about, if not actually feel, a great fear, and they were all talking at once and touching me as if I had only that very moment entered into life for the first time, and the miracle was shaking them from their complacent lives. I seemed to be the only one that knew that neither the death they had feared nor the birth they had felt carried with them any greater meaning than the deeply nurturing night of dreams and rest that I had passed while they suffered such changes.

There existed in that room, I realized later, a moment in which no movement at all could be perceived, and had I not witnessed the group of people on the other side of the room long before that moment, I would not have known they were alive. I might even have thought that the bars of light falling from the two holes in the ceiling were really poles placed there for some purpose I had not yet surmised but which had, most likely, something to do with climbing out. I had not yet, at that moment, imagined anyone wishing to remain in the room.

In time I realized it was no longer me they were talking about. I had been afraid of leaving such a world, and then I watched that world leave me. What I had thought was still, awaiting my actions, was moving forward, and it was I who had become still. The seductive hole I had once feared being placed in, back in that other life, which belonged to someone else, had slowly filled, and plants were growing from it while I had been walking away so slowly that the idea of it had caught up to me and then continued on, leaving me to imagine how much better those sad plants might have grown with a little more fertilizer nurturing their roots.

And the time came when the candles began dancing, and I wondered what event of Nature had now found its way through the two holes in the ceiling and affected the dense air holding the candle flames erect. Then I could see that the people across the room had begun dancing. They were moving in a slow languorous appreciation of each other's gestures that I wanted to describe as generous.

I watched them, thinking I was causing them deep anxiety at my inability to decide what would happen if I attempted to join them. And yet I chose instead to climb onto the table around which the candles were mounted and assert my authority and power, as none of them had done before me, by putting my two eyes to the two holes.

On the other side of those holes I saw another room, drenched in sunlight, with two shafts of darkness as solid as poles rising from the floor and a group of people talking in great animation and apparent pleasure while the shadows of leaves parted and swayed in clear definition like dark flames across the brilliant bright green table, at which a lone figure sat. I felt myself falling even before that figure stood and began to climb onto the table.

I knew then that I had been here before. I knew that the woman I had chosen to follow had also been here, but I did not know that that woman had been watching me, that she had selected me because of some mannerism or gesture in which she had placed value. Perhaps she could more easily merely select a man who appeared to her likely to make a choice she could not make herself, but I did not yet realize that she had anticipated my appearance and selected me because of this perception. Did this make her one of my kind or did this make me one of hers? I did not know.

It had not occurred to me that she was the only one watching. It had not occurred to me to wonder if she was really there.

BLUE OFFERING

I HADN'T SAID anything like this, nothing at all, to the long lost friend
I had found begging on the beach. We walked quietly, even his donkey
stepping slowly and carefully between the larger stones, as if afraid of waking
something, and the sound of the waves and the children seemed to excuse us.

I noticed branches discussing the wind and watched them startle a complacent
blue jay. His grip on the indifferent world released then. The sky was still there to
catch him, but what would it have to say to his trusting wings?

"I know myself well," my lost friend said, a proud contempt lighting his
sunken eyes. "And you, you know the way I was. That was when I began
my obsession with the blue comb. It contained stillness and more stillness,
and I thought I could find my happiness there." He spoke slowly, as if every
utterance risked calamity. Each sentence detoured around its own carefully
punctuated life.

And he rambled on in fits and starts about an old lover he had surprised on
the street, offering a glimpse here and a moment of silence there, and he spoke
of it as if it were happening again as he told me, but to someone else, someone
who had foolishly taken refuge in his body.

"I remember what it was that drew me. She always spoke so carefully, and
I looked for it again, as she talked and talked, until it was like she had killed
herself there in front of me. She had become a different person. My lover is

dead, and I must be kind to this new person, I said to myself, a witness who has lost much and grieves not."

I wondered if I too had died and gone as I watched the body left behind. I thought for a moment, but I didn't draw any conclusions.

And as if I had asked him a question in his silence, he continued, "Facts are useless. They do not know how to get around. Lies aren't so lonely."

He looked around as if expecting someone to be watching him, someone he may have feared. He looked at me as if trying to remember who I was, and then he pulled up the flap on the bag draped over his donkey's back and pulled out a bottle of beer and an opener. He opened the beer and put the opener and the bottle cap back in the bag and removed a bowl. I thought he was offering me something, and I was trying to figure out what, but he poured the beer in the bowl and set it down in front of the donkey, which could not have seen it otherwise because of the leather patches attached to his harness. The donkey kept his attention focused straight ahead, as if he were moving forward even as he stood there. The donkey drank the beer neatly and efficiently, paying no attention to either of us. He had been invited to a stranger's table.

"Every moment there are living things dying, and we breathe the escaping air until it escapes once more on its long journey away from us, but we still do not know where it's going." He said this staring sadly at the donkey's empty bowl.

I turned away from the falling sun, in the direction the wind had chosen for its last attack before giving up to the evening. It was that moment when you discover once more the long daily breath of your own shadow, and with the fall of the sun, the mood I had been experiencing all day fell as well, comfortably into place, no longer a shadow, and I enjoyed the alternative it provided to my lost friend's ant-like scuttling, and I rested, where I belonged, with the rising night and the creatures inside.

It was not until several days later that I realized I had not stopped thinking about the blue comb.

WILL YOU SHARE THE REST
OF YOUR LIFE WITH ME?

A PASSING TRAIN stirred the hot air. A breeze rushed across the tracks.
It lifted the man's long gray hair. The breeze set it down again. His vest
flapped. His tweed suit jacket, held like a waiter's linen over his arm, lifted
and fell neatly. I sat on a bench, sweating, nervously awaiting the arrival of the
woman I intended to marry.

The man waved to an odd little American woman with a deformity of her
right arm that made her rest it upon her left as she stood there, not seeing him
yet, offering the deformed arm with the odd posture of presentation she held,
as if she meant to give the arm away. In so doing, she created a small mirror
image of that portion of the man I had been focused upon as I imagined my
own gestures and posturing, trying to make real and desirable the invitation I
intended to present embody itself in a form of inevitability by seeing its every
detail as clearly as I could. The man seemed to be gesturing into the crowd
with his draped linen tweed jacket, just then stepping up to the platform.
He held a wrinkled sheaf of papers clutched in his left hand. Suddenly he
crumpled, slowly, almost methodically, as if he were folding his body away in
a drawer. The papers drifted across the planks towards me. I stepped towards
the fallen man. A conductor waiting nearby for an arriving train was already
at his side. I gathered the papers. They clung to my damp skin. Another train
arrived. Suddenly we were surrounded with passengers.

An ambulance appeared quickly, a link in a chain reaction. It seemed to be standing by, useless until its cue, impatient, blinking in the heat. Before I could penetrate the crowd, it flowed and opened on the other side of its own accord. The man was gone. I approached the conductor with the papers I had gathered. He gave me the man's name, Giorgi Stanevka. He had no other information and no address, but I held to the prospect of telling his story to my now late intended, who was of Russian extraction. The American woman had disappeared. I sat back down on the bench. I shuffled the dated pages into sequence. I began devouring them.

August 1, 1985:

A lie. Today the newspaper reported a plant had bloomed in Paris with "the largest flower ever known to have been produced in an artificial environment." The flower was three feet across and nine and a half feet tall. The paper reported the flower to be a "Giant Sumatran Morning Glory." That too is a lie. While it may describe the flower quite well and save the embarrassment of using its correct Latin name, amorphophallus titanum, even the poorly reproduced newspaper photograph is enough to reveal that the flower belongs to a magnificent but substantially smaller specimen of the plant which holds such importance in the tale I must now piece together. It concerns the family from which my wife may have descended and the odd circumstances and possibilities of her origins in a world which, for a few weeks in 1912 in a far province of eastern Russia, revolved around an elderly woman named Anna.

Even now as I gaze at Sergei Mikhailovich Prokudin-Gorskii's photograph of this woman named Anna, I long for a proper end to her story. My young wife (young to me, at 83, though she has survived 72 years herself) bears, at times, an uncanny resemblance to Anna as she appears in the 1912 photograph. The resemblance lends a certain comforting timelessness to these thoughts.

My wife's personal history remains shrouded in many mysteries, but she is certain that her mother lived in Izvedovo shortly before she gave birth to a daughter. My wife and I met in London thirty-two years ago, both of us having suffered through miserable first marriages that lasted far longer than they should have out of some misguided sentiments about the sanctity of marriage. My wife's mother, it is said, died before my wife was yet a full year old, and she knows nothing at all of her father. She was raised in foster homes in St. Petersburg,

Warsaw, and finally Paris, where she met her first husband.

I think of this now because I have just this day received word that my daughter will any day give birth late in life to a daughter of her own. I fear I shall not be here to relate these events to her directly. I approach death even now as my granddaughter approaches life, with far too little knowledge to fully understand or appreciate what is to come.

Evening of August 3, 1985:

Before the revolution, the village of Izvedovo had been left in obscurity, and few Russians, to say nothing of foreigners, had ever seen it. In 1912, however, an auspicious event took place. The village was visited by Sergei Mikhailovich Prokudin-Gorskii, an esteemed chemist, photographer and artist, who had been commissioned by Czar Nicholas II to document Russian life with his photographs, some, for the first time, done in color. No one seems to remember the exact day he came, and in fact the man stayed for barely a week, but all agree it was in midsummer. And all agree the most memorable moment of his stay was the sitting of Anna Yevtusko for her photograph. When asked what might best portray the life of the village, it was agreed by the villagers that a photograph of Anna at her spinning wheel would best hold on film, or glass plates, as it was done in 1912, the unique character of their lives.

Anna herself took the event in stride and continued her spinning whenever Sergei was not asking her to hold still. She was pleased to have been chosen for this attention, but when one of the children watching said, "It's magic," her reply was, "There are many kinds of magic, child."

As with most of the villagers, Anna's entire life had been spent in the same village, and she had left only once, a pilgrimage including visits to the ancient Church of the Ogiditria Virgin and the Verkhoture Monastery (both of which were also photographed by Sergei) where she visited Abbot Xenophon. Sasha Kantinski, the only English-speaking resident of the village, claims that the sense of austerity and reverence attendant upon Anna's selection for the photograph remains as brilliant as crystal in her memory, and she has carried it with her all her long life.

Seventy-three years later, I sit here in my study, half a world away, and gaze at the finally published photographs of Sergei Mikhailovich Prokudin-Gorskii with a certain misplaced nostalgia. For this is not my own history, and yet I believe anyone would have a similar sense of reverence gazing upon Anna's photograph, as many apparently did when it was first shown in Paris in 1923. Anna's fingers seem to hold the fibers so lightly, with such obvious sensitivity, and the lines in her face express such care, such concern, that the viewer feels as if this attention were being bestowed upon him and invests himself in the strands of fiber she holds. The entire photograph carries an expressive blue-gray tint, and the details of the hand-hewn wooden porch and Anna's home-spun clothing express a warmth which is difficult to even imagine and impossible for me to express with the eloquence of that photograph.

It is with a deep affection and warmth then that these pictures have held me in their sway over the course of the last few days, and yet, with the inevitability of time, I am drawn on now to the events that followed the photographer's visit.

After decades of quiet rural life, Izvedovo was visited within the course of one summer not only by the esteemed Sergei Mikhailovich Prokudin-Gorskii, but by the most unusual accumulation of traveling human oddities to my knowledge ever assembled in rural Russia, or perhaps anywhere. The Kobelkoff Carnival, led by Nikolai Kobelkoff, known professionally as The Armless and Legless Wonder, came to Izvedovo scarcely one month after Sergei Mikhailovich Prokudin-Gorskii had departed.

The village met the visitors with an odd assortment of responses. Curiosity and revulsion, of course, were to be expected, and the troupe would have met with no success whatsoever in their travels without such reliable human reactions to deformity and excess. But there was, too, an odd sense of homecoming, perhaps attendant upon the similarities of life in such an isolated setting to the equally isolating physical peculiarities of the members of the carnival. As with the manufactured excitements and artificial attentions the carnival members were in the business of stimulating, the exaggerated attentions felt by the villagers during the recent unusual events in Izvedovo encouraged an odd compression of time.

August 14, 1985:

Every witness I have been able to locate to these events, which I intend to relate here, remembers them as if they encompassed several years instead of only a few weeks. Anna Yevtusko did not, of course, approve of the carnival, with its bedraggled entourage of roustabouts, ne'er-do-wells and thieves, but several of its featured attractions seemed to have caught at her heartstrings and she took to visiting the carnival at teatime. She, perhaps more than anyone else, seemed

disturbed by the spotlight that had of late been turned upon the village, and her
teatime visits may have been partly an attempt to deflate the differences between
the villagers and the carnival troupe. Her appearance did, in fact, take much of
the sideshow freaks-on-display atmosphere away from the carnival encampment,
and those who were gawking at the attractions were invited to sit down instead
to tea and participate in a civilized discussion of the astonishing varieties of tea
leaves, or the unique character of Russian rural history, or the family lineage of any
respectable citizen of Izvedovo.

Fortunately, the carnival troupe quickly grew fond of Anna and did not resent
the infringement upon their usual means of livelihood. Anna encouraged the
villagers to provide for the new guests and even in some cases to hire them, but she
could not succeed in dispelling the general understanding that this was to be only a
temporary, if welcome, change for the carnival troupe.

There were those who conjectured that the village's past history had something
to do with Anna's desire to take these new friends into the fold, for it was rumored
that the village had ostracized Siamese twins and left them to die on nearby Mt.
Kucheskoi during Anna's youth, but most simply gave credit where it was due, to
the warmth and kindness of the village's generous matriarch.

August 15, 1985:

I realize now that the carnival was an historical oddity as well, for it was
probably the most comprehensive assemblage of human exceptions the world
has yet witnessed. Several entrepreneurs of circus and sideshow acts, including
P.T. Barnum and Buffalo Bill, had brought great public attention and a new
means of support to such human oddities in the late 19th century in the U.S. and
Europe, and several of the better known acts had tired of the grueling pace and
exploitation of such profiteers. Led by the Russian Armless and Legless Wonder,
Nikolai Kobelkoff, they had banded together to tour the world and enjoy life at a
more leisurely pace. Perhaps Kobelkoff had convinced them his native homeland
was the place to start. Or perhaps the hope of catching up with Sergei Mikhailovich
Prokudin-Gorskii played a part in their decision to visit Izvedovo, but nothing in
my research points to any serious likelihood of truth in the latter speculation. My
thoughts now turn as well to the risks of speculation, but let me assure you that
I have spent many years researching these events and if the past cannot be fully
discovered, it can be imagined with a vigilant allegiance to probability.

And so I must report that there were no less than thirteen featured attractions heralding the Kobelkoff Carnival. There was Hans Langseth, a Norwegian and a physically normal human being except for a beard that measured, at that time, fourteen feet two inches and reached seventeen feet six inches before his death in 1927. The beard is now on display in the Smithsonian Institute. And there was Laloo, a Mohammedan, who had a small twin, minus the head, attached to his breastbone, and traveled with his physically normal wife. And there were the Tocci Brothers, twins sharing the same body from the sixth rib down but possessing two heads and two distinctly separate personalities. Each of them had a wife, one Italian, one Polish, also traveling with the troupe. And there was Prince Randian, "The Living Torso," armless and legless like Kobelkoff, his torso small and thin compared to his fully formed head, also known as "The Caterpillar Man," traveling with his wife and four children. And there was James Morris, "The Elastic Skin Man," who could raise the skin of his chest to the top of his head, cover one leg with the skin of the other, and pull his cheeks out a full eight inches, and who also was, however, a hopeless, if amusing, drunk. And there were, as well, many less unusual oddities doubling as carnival laborers and other help, including a monstrously fat woman and her seriously thin husband, several midget acrobats, a sword swallower, and a fire-eater.

Despite these attractions, it has been reported, it took little more than a week for Anna to replace the carnival atmosphere with the more "normal" routines of her own rural life, but could the performers exist happily without the habitual excitement of being on display?

August 16, 1985:

The second week, it appears, began with the usual tea visits from Anna and a dwindling entourage of locals, but it was becoming apparent that Kobelkoff was already getting a little restless. The conversation had stumbled more than once before Kobelkoff chanced upon Anna's interest in herbs and medicinal plants. Notes were compared. Arguments ensued and were generally settled agreeably, though both Kobelkoff and Anna were said to have snickered in disbelief at each other's sometimes elevated claims for the curative powers of certain botanicals. The evening soon grew past dusk, and Anna's entourage had long since disappeared when the conversation that must have occurred finally ended, but since Anna lived alone in a cottage at the edge of the village, no one really knew how far the

relationship developed that night. Looking back now with Anna's photograph in
my hands, I like to think that the respect my thoughts of Anna arouse is based, not
unreasonably, on the kindness I discern in her manner and photograph, radiating
from the experiences of an intelligent woman, unafraid of the risks of emotional
generosity under any circumstances. And I am convinced that such a woman,
even at Anna's probably somewhat advanced age, is fully capable of welcoming the
experience of bearing a child. No one seems to know that age with any certainty,
an elder often being much less advanced in those days than is the case now, when
people routinely live so much longer.

Anna's entourage swelled to a rather large crowd the next day for the usual
teatime visit due to Kobelkoff's mischievous placement of a rumor that, in
response to Anna's botanical interests, he would display from his private collection
a rare specimen of the plant world at teatime. Conversation began as usual,
with remarks upon the weather and other mundane observations inflaming the
impatience of those who had accompanied Anna solely for the prospect of viewing
an exceedingly rare plant. As the visit progressed, Kobelkoff's comments and
attentions became more and more directed to Anna, and there were those who
claimed an edge of intimacy existed between Kobelkoff and Anna even in these
exceedingly botanical exchanges.

Having no arms or legs, Kobelkoff naturally satisfied most of his physical
needs for expression and mobility with either the assistance of others or with his
mouth, and in due course, Kobelkoff signaled with a bell he rang with his teeth
to a carnival roustabout, and a small wagon with a large box on top was wheeled
out into the midst of the assembled onlookers. One side of the box was glass so that
viewing of the botanical specimen could be accomplished without opening the box.

Kobelkoff then shocked the assemblage by referring to the gigantic flower
as "The Engorged Member" instead of its legitimate Latinate appendage,
amorphophallus titanum. Nervous laughter awkwardly escaped the witnesses.

The flower had, as well, somewhat the appearance of a gigantic upturned
"morning glory" at least four feet across. The rim was deeply fluted with ruffled
edges, and an enormous yellow protuberance arose from the middle, which
was lined with deep maroon. Kobelkoff explained that the box was rigged
with vertical bellows extenders because the plant, which was taller than any
of the onlookers could reach, over twelve feet in height, was still growing. He
explained the need to enclose the plant, due to its origins in the hot humid
climate of Sumatra. This particular specimen had been acquired from a

London botanist who had propagated a specimen stolen from London's famed Kew Gardens. Kobelkoff had owned it for nearly five years, and this was the first time it had bloomed. Since there was no way of knowing how long the bloom might last, he had wanted everyone to see it. Some said its display was really a lover's gift for Anna, who sat enthralled and speechless as Kobelkoff pontificated upon its unusual nature and lineage. As it was, for that region of Russia, a rather hot and humid day, Kobelkoff consented to very briefly opening a small panel in the case. All who stood nearby agreed that the plant emitted a powerful stench not unlike a mixture of burnt sugar and rotten fish that very quickly attracted numerous flies.

For the next three days the flower was on constant display and Anna shared in the educational aspects of presenting the unusual specimen to the increasing number of travelers who had heard, God only knows how (though Kobelkoff must have had his showman's understanding of publicity at work in one way or another), about the unusual new arrival in Izvedovo. A few of the carnival troupe were troubled by the degree to which their own abilities and unusual attributes had been eclipsed by first an ordinary woman and then a plant, but they mostly kept quiet for the sake of Anna and Kobelkoff. The blooming giant caused such excitement that no one seemed to notice if Anna, who had become a nearly permanent fixture at the plant's side, returned to her cottage that night. A rural village the size of Izvedovo would not normally miss such an occasion for potential gossip, but the excitement over the flower had grown larger than any interest in Anna's personal life, at least temporarily.

August 17, 1985:

Anna insisted upon the botanical education of every visitor to the exceedingly rare display of the unique specimen entrusted, if only temporarily, to her care and steadfastly refused to allow Kobelkoff to charge an admission fee, though she did allow contributions, but only to the extent of the costs of feeding the carnival troupe during their non-profit stay in Izvedovo.

(The page was here torn, and I descended from my humble seated throne (for the privilege of entering the world of this lofty lie did make me feel and even speak thus) and explored the teeming platform as carefully as I could without appearing to be searching for coins or discarded tobacco remnants.

As I did so, I reveled in the exaggerated postures I found myself taking upon my bearing as I combed unsuccessfully the landscape of the platform, and all too quickly grew anxious to get back to the story.)

August 19, 1985:

It was a time of excitement and peaceful coexistence unsurpassed in the history of Izvedovo. Not only did the locals and the carnival troupe get along so well one would swear they had all been friends for years, but domestic violence, drunken brawls, and even accidents in the field, all fell to virtual extinction. And Anna, in her intoxicating educational enthusiasm and botanical goodwill, virtually blossomed herself, alongside the now famous plant. Everyone I've been able to contact, who had been in Izvedovo at the time, remembers that summer with a tremendous sense of peace and luminous health.

But, of course, the bloom faded and died, and the plant itself began looking sickly. Kobelkoff decided it was time to dig the plant up and divide the corm (a tuberous root similar to an iris bulb, Anna explained, in one of her botanical lectures), and the result was no less than six smaller corms. Two of these were encased in wood and glass just like the original and left in Anna's care. The remaining four went with Kobelkoff, for it had now become apparent that the carnival troupe had grown too restless and would soon leave without him if Kobelkoff did not give the order to break camp and move on. James Morris, "The Elastic Skin Man," had already slipped out of camp on two different occasions and frightened the locals in three nearby villages with drunken skin stretching demonstrations and, it was rumored, spent the night with a young rebellious virgin who later had a daughter with normal skin.

Anna could not, despite her obvious attraction to Kobelkoff, bring herself to leave Izvedovo. Her home, her friends, her sense of being respected, her entire life, were in Izvedovo, and not even Kobelkoff could change that.

The entire village turned out for a celebration honoring the unique plant in which it was determined that the tuber alone weighed just over one hundred and four pounds, but the stem and flower had already begun wilting and could not be accurately measured. The soon-to-be-dormant tuber was ceremonially reburied in fresh soil, lightly dampened and well-fertilized, with all due pomp and circumstance. Most understood, too, that this was really a going-away party for the carnival troupe, and the carnival did leave Izvedovo the very next day.

August 20, 1985:

Rumor has it, of course, that Kobelkoff returned several times to visit Anna, but if so, it was in secret, for no one I've spoken with has been able to say for sure that they ever saw them together again after that time. Rumor has it, too, that a rare specimen of the Brazilian "Pelican Flower" was delivered to Anna's cottage in a carefully sealed wooden box from London. No one seems very sure that this too was not romantic wishful thinking. The description circulating with the rumor, at least as far as I have been able to verify it in botanical reference works, of the "Pelican Flower" as having "the appearance of a large mottled handkerchief put out on the bushes to dry" is accurate however. Whoever started the rumor seems clearly to have seen one somewhere.

Still another rumor based on a photograph of a small child sitting on a gigantic water-lily pad in Holland at the Van Houtte Gardens in a conservatory built specially to house the giant waterlilies claims that a woman in the background of the photograph is Anna. Although I have been able to verify that the Kobelkoff Carnival did pass near the Van Houtte Gardens, I have not been able to prove that the time of this passing coincided with a possible absence from Izvedovo by Anna or that the dates of the Van Houtte Garden's giant water-lily display could have encompassed the probable dates of the Kobelkoff Carnival's visit to Holland. An enlargement of the photograph hangs now in my study but does nothing to prove or disprove this rumor. There are times when I imagine that the figure in the photograph is Anna, and the resemblance seems clear. And equally, there are times when I am convinced that it could not be her.

I too have done my research. All the characters of the tale are real. The flowers are real. The carnival characters did indeed exist and travel about displaying themselves to make a living, and the years in which they did it could have coincided to allow them to form the troupe. But there is no record of such travels in Russia although the photographer existed and made the first color photographs of rural Russia in the applicable years. More than one of them includes a woman who could have been Anna, but no other record of Anna or her complete name exists. The locations in which the events are purported to have taken place are all real. So much of the story is real that I begin to feel that only my own life is in doubt.

The last page is torn at the bottom, cutting off what may have been a closing date or yet another entry, the month beginning impossibly with what appears to be a scrawling J. I turn from that last crumpled page of the story, and I see Anna, not just in the face of the American woman who disappeared long ago now from the train platform, but in the faces of all the passing women of my life. I try to read the experience in their eyes. I yearn to offer them exotic flowers and tell them stories, like this one I still hold in my hands so many years later. Sometimes, for a while, they might believe the stories, but when they leave, and they will leave as I must leave, as we all must, I will wish them well and miss them, searching for another who is, of course, the same.

I brush back my hair. I fold my useless jacket over my arm. But I will not yet fold my body away. And I will step away from the passing trains. Now, after my waiting here has rewarded me with nothing else, I can give you only my life as I find it in these damp pages, and in Giorgi, his heart collapsed (for the conductor reported his death) in that past so persistently present, where my own heart lingers like a voyeur, incomplete, a murmur in the life of a dead man. I belong there, in a different time and place, now that it has become clear the woman whose hands I intended to place my life in is not going to arrive as I had expected. Why else would one with nowhere to go have waited so long upon a train platform?

I have become a murmur risen from the wooden throne of a waiting area pew. I step forward out of the past onto the empty platform to kneel there, alone, and ask the passing trains, Can the memory of a woman who cannot receive me sustain my life?

THAT NIGHT HIS FATHER

A MAN LIMPS in the distance, the reverent blue of a cloudless sky framing his hunch and drag forward into the glittering morning of something like gossip dancing from the broken glass on the ridge above the garbage dump.

Torn drapes, a window-shade, a washtub and bucket, ears of seed-corn strung on a wire in the attic . . . Her soapy fingers linger in the dishwater as she watches him.

His thoughts turn back to a room where the lights from the highway traveled slowly across the wall. The barn creaked in the wind, and the wind made that night his new father. Listen, it said, to the wheel turning inside you. Nothing is easier to understand than loss.

An apple basket, a bag of grain, two tin plates and a broken fork, spring-water in a tin cup, trees wet with darkness and a broken window with tattered lace curtains.

The soft thunder of blackbirds landing on the roof. For a moment this is the Russian countryside, a light at dusk in the parlor. Unexpected, a knock on the door. Cautiously, they give you the bad news.

BLUE THEATER MADE OF FIELDS AND MIRRORS

1.

THE DIRECTOR pokes his head out from between two curtains.

Silence.

He disappears then reappears in the same manner.

Silence.

This happens several times. Each time he seems to gain a little more confidence, but he remains suspicious. Finally he comes out from behind the curtain and peers into the darkness a couple of times. He screws up his face and makes a difficult and meaningful adjustment of his facial muscles.

Silence.

"Look, I'm in charge here."

Silence.

Another difficult and meaningful adjustment of facial muscles.

Silence.

A faint light reveals a blue person of indeterminate gender sitting motionless and calm. The director, feigning authority, walks slowly, suspiciously, over to the motionless blue person. He folds his hands behind his back and strolls in a circle. He reaches back with his hand as if he were going to slap the blue person's face.

The blue person remains motionless.

The director pokes the blue person with his index finger as if to determine what he/she is made of.

Silence.

The director strides purposefully away, conspicuously ignoring the blue person. He explores the stage, peering into floor cracks, staring at the ceiling, sighting along the edge of the stage to see how unfair it is. Gradually he works his way back to the blue person and continues this method on him/her. He shows more curiosity about his new victim than he did about the walls, the floor, or the ceiling, but his interest is disguised. It is possible that some of this is developing into mild amusement, but it is difficult to determine just how amusing such a situation could be.

Finally the director says, "You know something? You're really blue."

Silence.

The director wanders off, vaguely curious, examining. He arrives at the place where the two curtains meet. He seems interested. He pokes his head between, pulls back, wanders off. He returns to the curtains, pokes his head between. A bulge can be seen wandering back and forth. After a while the bulge is gone.

The blue person remains motionless.

Silence continues rehearsing.

2.

You assume it was human. You question the victims accordingly. Under the glare of the spotlight, they begin to suspect their motives. Just as you are about to imprison them in your confession, one of them gathers up his confusion and admits that nothing happened.

Disguising your failure in parables, you promise to stop pressuring him, but of course you are lying. You realize you are outnumbered. You tell them to turn around, face the height chart. Slowly, you read them their numbers. You allow them to consider building churches.

You make a point of enjoying your cigarette. As long as they do not realize there is nothing to keep them from smoking, you have a chance.

3.

Once upon a time, a used thought salesman was pacing in the parking lot, minding your own business. A man in a crumpled trenchcoat hit you in the face with his wallet and said, "See that? I'm a detective. I don't want to be nosey, but my wife wants to know what you were doing the night of July 4 between 10 AM and 3 PM and give me a light for my cigar, will you?"

You remember thinking about putting your lighter in the inside pocket of your coat but deciding, for some reason you can no longer remember, not to.

"Can I give you my card?" you ask, hoping for a diversion.

"Could I get you to sign it? My wife collects 'em. The kids are crazy about her stroganoff."

You take a card from your back pocket. You reach inside your coat for a pen and the unused thought you find there opens its doors and explodes as you step inside.

The detective pokes in the ashes until he finds a small flame. He lights his cigar.

4.

Okay, so the man's a comedian, then. People should laugh at him. His partner is a plant (hold up plant). His partner is not here. People should laugh at him. He does things to his dog (hold up dog) with a fork (hold up fork).

Think about the dog (hold up dog). What is his relationship with the plant (hold up plant)? Who writes all the jokes? Is the plant (hold up plant) as funny at home as it is on stage? Is the dog (hold up dog) jealous of the plant's (hold up plant) fame? What is the significance of the fork (hold up fork)?

Be sure to water (never try to hold up water) your plant (hold up plant) regularly, and a little chopped, hard-boiled egg (hold up soft semi-ovoid sphere of gelatinous white nurturing matter surrounding a heat-solidified chicken fetus, sufficiently cooled so as not to burn your fingers) wouldn't hurt.

So you come to the conclusion that there is something disturbing in your partner's inability to laugh. Jealousy is not funny. And the recent upsurge in the acceptance of dog spooning (hold up spoon, hold up dog) in Southern California explains nothing.

Why does the director (hold out right arm, point at a man in the audience) never laugh (hold out left arm, turn quickly at right angle, slapping palm of hand across mouth) at such emptiness?

5.

Again a man appears on the stage. This man might be funny. He's leading a wimpy little wiener dog. People should laugh at him. The man's partner is a plant. People should laugh at him. He sets down his partner like a gift. He does gentle things to his dog with a fork. People should laugh at them.

Is the man who might be funny really funny? What is his obligation in regard to the plant? How can an audience learn to appreciate cruelty if they don't laugh? Why has the man's identity been kept a secret from the man?

So K. has a bomb in his suitcase, next to the wooden dummy, and K. is a comedian.

Will the bomb, the joke, or K.'s life go off?

Let us assume, for the sake of argument, that K. is a sad man. It's funnier that way. Perhaps K.'s life has no meaning. Would the laughter create a meaning if one did not already exist?

6.

Central to any deeper understanding of the man's character would be the man's lack of humor. And so a woman dressed in white slithered past the two prospective patients. Smirked. Loudly. She picked up a copy of Mr. Molar's Tooth Tips for Tots, Chainsaw Commandos, The Hardy Boys Bust a Gut, Ten Reasons to Dress Your Husband in Blue, and A Treatise Concerning Unnatural Sex Practices Among Circus Performers.

"That's me," said the friendly dwarf actor with a toothache to Ed Sullivan's brother-in-law, who wasn't sure which of the woman's selected reading materials he was pointing at.

A comedian arrived at the dentist's office with a false aralia. His tooth hurt. He took a number and sat down to discuss the dog spooning routine with his plant.

"Twenty-three," a voice said, "number twenty-three, please."

"Maybe it would be funnier with a butter knife," said the comedian.

The woman dressed in white put her blindfold back on and returned A Treatise Concerning Unnatural Sex Practices Among Circus Performers to the magazine rack. On the way back to her seat, she turned off the light over the fish tank, slipped Mr. Molar's Tooth Tips for Tots into her handbag, and began whistling loudly. Something like The Love Theme from Romeo and Juliet or Stairway to Heaven.

"That's a false aralia, isn't it," said the woman dressed in white, suddenly removing her blindfold.

"Yes," said the comedian, "but he prefers being called an aralia."

"I can understand that," said the woman dressed in white. "My son is in Vietnam."

"What does he do there?" asked the comedian. Casually. Making conversation. Counting ordinaries.

"He shoots craps, snakes, Vietnamese, and heroin," said the woman dressed in white.

"I don't think that's very funny," said the comedian.

The comedian got up to go to the bathroom and put his partner on the table. When he got back, the woman was laughing.

"I'm a comedian," said the comedian.

"That's pretty funny," said the woman.

7.

The play takes place in the basement of a large brick building so you descend a curving staircase with cement on all sides. By the time you reach the doorway with the black curtains instead of a door, your legs have gone rubbery, so you quickly sit down near the stage in the darkened theater. Even before you catch your breath, the lights come on, and they spill across the stage past your chair into the second or third row. You turn around to discover no one else in the theater. You hear voices, and the play seems to be taking place on the other side of the blood red stage curtain.

Soon enough the lights go down and the actors, dressed as theater attendants, enter stage left with flashlights, directing several ticket holders to your row. The last of the ticketholders, sitting in the lap of another ticketholder sitting in the lap of another, hands you a red coffee can filled with night crawlers just as the lights come on. You can read "The Natural Way" on the side of the coffee can. Then a flashlight beam insults you, an usher you assume, so you move toward it, and it begins moving away from you. You begin running after the light, afraid of what's required of you, and suddenly you pass through curtains into a brightly lit hallway. You reach back through the curtain to verify the past, but there is a door, locked, where you assumed before there had been only curtains.

Softly echoing down a hallway to the right, you hear applause, laughter. You follow the hallway a very long time. The applause guides you. Finally you despair of ever arriving and enter a second doorway, draped, like the first, in black cloth. Again you find your way to a stage, but this time you cannot consider choosing which row to be seated in because there is only one. Expecting more actors dressed as ushers to appear, you decide to rush the first one, wrestle him to the cement floor and question him. You no longer find enigmas entertaining. A soft whoosh of air passes before you, and slowly you can see candles beginning to glow warmly in a line across the stage, each one softly hiding behind a paper bag. You inspect the nearest bag, and it is partly filled with sand, the candle fat and scented with vanilla, anchored in the sand. No actors appear. You sit, determined to discover the meaning of all this with your patience. Years later, as the candles go out, you notice the glow of a black light calling out neon green arrows, which have appeared next to each of the bags. You follow the arrows until you again enter a brightly lit hallway. You reach back through the curtains, and your knuckles rap suddenly against brick. Far down the hallway, the sound of distant laughter, distant applause.

8.

Now the stage is the world. This world is an island, but we are not alone there. The tip of the stage rises to a cliff where a celebration is taking place. There is dancing like an old Celtic fair with Maypoles and women with ribbons in their hair. But this is a modern celebration, and you can rent small balloon propulsion-packs that will lift you above the crowds and let you steer them against the winds rising up across the cliff from the ocean.

As you turn your balloon into the wind to watch the dancing from above, you notice immediately the ringlets of a thin woman's red hair, accented by a crown of twigs and ribbon for the dancing, and you remember the freckles speckled across the bridge of her nose. Where have you seen here before? You angle the balloon lower, closer to the earth, and a gust of wind slams the balloon hard. You cannot hold your position and barely manage to escape injury as the wind presses you to the earth. For a moment you are held there by the wind as she looks, startled, at this clumsy man trying to fly. Then the wind changes, and your balloon leaps into the air, dragging you away like a nervous child would pull away a puppy sniffing a stranger's hand.

Late, earthbound, the curtain of rain that scattered the dancers and ended your flight suddenly disperses and you find her red hair in the crowd on the beach. Then twilight and the two of you walk without speaking, uncertain how to begin touching. A loud rushing noise startles you. Expecting a boat or perhaps a whale, we turn (Forgive me for joining you—it's a dream and we represent, of course, the same person) towards the ocean. A submarine rises from the sea, and one by one, a dozen large light bulbs pop out of the hatch and float toward us. They form a raft at the shoreline like a large piece of bubble-wrap, and we are helpless to resist. How did they convince us to climb on? How do we resist trying to pop them?

They take us to the submarine, and we climb down into a room where a large table is set for what appears to be a Thanksgiving dinner. Several light bulbs are already seated around the table, as well as two pairs of ordinary looking middle-class human beings. Are they supposed to be our parents? As the light bulbs enter the hatch, they stretch like glass softened in a very hot flame and do not return to their light bulb shapes for several minutes. They may be able to move through very small openings this way.

You reach for the food, but the aliens are holding back your hands. You can smell the food, and you are very hungry, but the aliens do not release your hands. The redhead looks to see if you are watching her, the food, or the aliens. Her lips move, but there is no sound inside the submarine. Next to the turkey lies an oven mitt shaped like a turkey, heavily padded. It stands up and opens its oven mitt beak. The redhead's mouth opens, and from the look in her eyes, you understand the aliens opened it. The oven mitt turkey picks caraway seeds, one at a time, from a large piece of French bread and places them at the back of her tongue. Then it is your turn.

This takes a very long time, and it is all we are allowed to eat. When we are finished eating caraway seeds, our new alien surrogate parents say, in unison, "It is very satisfying to watch our children making love." There is no sound in the submarine. You turn to see if she has understood this. She looks puzzled but no longer frightened. The light bulbs turn on and off as if in applause, and they continue applauding as they float us back to the shore where yet another new world awaits its stage.

9.

When you overhear your husband's anger at a trip to the store for light bulbs, you know the time has come. You dash down the street to the only neighbor left who will listen to you complain, and you begin drilling holes

in the sidewalk. He nearly catches you, but the telltale backfire of his ancient
Buick is unmistakable, and you begin playing on the lawn, the drill cradled
between like a baby. He wants to remove you from the lawn, but lawns belong
to everyone.

Dusk arrives with a flare of bats darting under the streetlight where the
insects gather. He's humming inside, moving light bulbs from one socket to
another. He is trying to arrange them so they will burn out at the same time.

You want to wake up now, and you do. Your husband is slicing cheese for
the finicky grandmother of twenty. She leaves honey in his mailbox.

10.

You say hello to the fluffy snowstorm, and a shape seems to form between
the trees. You move closer, and it moves deeper into the woods.

Some people spend a lifetime in these woods. Some of them are crazy. Some
of them are happy, and cannot explain why. They simply smile and point.

You are a responsible citizen, so you listen. Smile and point.

Behind you another car stops on the highway. A helpful human being or
another lost soul?

Can you see my shape between the trees?

And then the sound of brakes as the travelers come suddenly upon the
evidence. Why are these cars stopped, empty, purring on the roadside?

11.

The director wanders on to the stage, which is humming with lunchtime
activity; tables and trays and food and conversation. No one notices him until
a blue man of indeterminate gender enters stage left and slowly, lingeringly,
buys a can of pop from a pop machine while searching the cafeteria with an
angry domineering glare. The director moves toward the angry figure like
a ghost, but the blue man sees him, and as the director reaches the vending
machine, the stage goes silent. The two of them continue their dance in the
spotlight, as if choreographed, hitting each other repeatedly with rubber light
bulbs.

The spotlight fades, and the actors adjust their chairs at their tables, so that
they can see each other while they eat their lunch. The lights fade. A spotlight
pierces the auditorium, revealing, yes, your bedroom. You are preparing for

sleep. The show is about to begin. Your fears are no longer visible.

As your eyes close, the actors begin applauding. Only two seats, far in the back of the auditorium, are occupied One contains you, the other a puppet with a loud smile frozen on its wooden face. The puppet begins emitting a soft blue glow. You cannot know when you will stop.

A MISUNDERSTANDING

"THE POSSUM is sleeping," said the possum's mother to the possum's father.

"But we're possums too," interjected the possum's father. Pipe smoke circled his head like a ghostly bird about to roost.

"Not unless we're sleeping," reasoned the possum's mother. "Have you not seen the evidence decorating the roadways along which so many creatures travel?"

"Oh those things. They come from the tiny white eggs produced by tortured Gods," said the possum's father, puffing away.

"I didn't fall off the turnip truck yesterday," said the possum's mother.

"Well at the moment you're thinking about it, your past is the present. So it's not the past. You can only have a past if you don't think about it. If somebody else does. But then you don't know you have a past," said the possum's pompous father.

"I don't have to do anything to be here. But unless I think about it, how do I know I'm here? But if I think about it, I'm no longer here, I'm in my thoughts about being here," countered the possum's mother with a touch of irritation in her voice. She paused, then added, "Please don't upset the child."

"When I saw them along the road like that, it was an experience so sensual it was almost repugnant, like cottage cheese. It was the moon's wet touch sticking to you like insect parts," added the possum's father, pausing to look closely at the possum's mother before adding, "I don't think you were in that experience. I don't think you were there where I was having that happen to me."

Air was all over the place. You could breathe it without thinking twice. Clearly, it was taken for granted.

"You're like a child who likes to pull the wings off of angels. But if there ever was an angel who couldn't fly, it's you." That's really what she said, the possum's mother.

The possum's father didn't answer. He was reading an obituary he had found on the wings of a fly. He was quite sure it wasn't his, or he wouldn't have been talking about it.

The thoughts keeping them apart were interrupted by the unmistakable sputter of a foreign god passing. It was the roadster responsible for the casualties along the pathway to enlightenment.

Let it go.

But if there is no place to stop, why must we?

PAUL KLEE'S ILLEGITIMATE GRANDSON CONSIDERS THE EVIDENCE CONCERNING HIS DECEASED BROTHER'S LITERARY INTENTIONS

1.

CHAPTER THE FIRST, as outlined repeatedly with not a word's variation, in which the hero of the planned but never written novel, Sylvester, denies any knowledge, biblical or otherwise, of our heroine, Janice, and the public television special Opossums and Their Kind is paraphrased as a subplot to the beginning of the great flood.

2.

In which the great desert would be established as a belabored analogy for the difficulties of life in deprivation, here defined as a derth of satellite dishes and lime gummy bears. Cacti of impressive diversity provide lengthy digression and documentary backgrounds of stark realism for the dance of the wounded bumblebee, which ends the chapter.

3.

In which would be set forth in almost documentary forthrightness and detail the mating habits of the common housefly.

4.

In which a virtual *Cinema Verité* of painfully detailed graphic intensity will offer for examination the evidence of the first corpse, upon which lands, to end the chapter, two common houseflies. One is left to assume they are of opposing gender.

5.

In which objectivity is repeatedly tortured while bound and gagged during an incomprehensibly lengthy encounter with yet another ordinary insect. In keeping with the chapter's purposeful evasions, no judgment is passed, and no assumptions are implied. Following the surprisingly intense and lyrical description of the insect's gestation, the fully realized ant emerges from beneath an abandoned peanut butter and jelly sandwich but is unable to proceed beyond the slick vertical edges of the bowl in which the sandwich resides. A tour de force of innuendo emerging from three crucial plot questions cascades from the abrupt cliff of implicit refusal, which the narrative has carefully established.

1. Who has abandoned the peanut butter and jelly sandwich and why?
2. Why is the ant, a social creature if there ever was one, alone?
3. Is the narrative sufficiently devoid of human intentions to fully dissuade the reader from questioning the narrator's motives, or have we entered the mind of a character relentlessly evading his or her own personal difficulties while nevertheless establishing that he/she has the sensitivity to have some?

6.

In which the leg of an animal of indeterminate species, all too possibly human, is seen to be sinking slowly into the mire. Mud-streaked curlicues of blonde hair form a pattern of half-moons and question marks as the leg holds momentarily, just at the surface, then descends into the seething primal fecundity of nature's overwhelming will.

7.

In which the construction of a gourd banjo is related to the taut anticipation of murder.

8.

In which our hero resurfaces to eat a peanut butter and jelly sandwich.

9.

In which our heroine resurfaces to go jogging along a suspicious path, which weaves its way through forest, meadow and swamp. Someone other than our hero observes her.

10.

In which Sylvester selects a hat. Thirty-three pages in thirty-three styles. Sylvester cannot choose. The clerk insists upon the white cowboy hat. In this insistence we detect the clerk's inordinate need for protection.

11.

In which a bizarre accident involving peanut brittle in the candy factory in which she works takes the life of Janice's mother.

12.

In which Sylvester views a popular movie mystery in the privacy of his own home and concludes that it could never have happened. Which attracts Sylvester a great deal since it evocatively duplicates how he feels about his own life.

13.

In which several young gentlemen of indeterminate means and questionable character offer their services for no apparent reason to the government. Their motivations appear not to be relevant. It's not their story. By contrast, the hero and heroine now appear to be more fully realized.

14.

In which Sylvester dreams of the sea and adds several new specimens to his admirable butterfly collection.

15.

In which Janice declines a heartfelt offer of membership in *The Society for the Prevention of the Future* and cans several jars of huckleberry jam.

16.

In which Janice is once more jogging through forest, meadow and marsh, observed by a suspicious unidentified figure. She locates the pebble hiding in her running shoe and carefully observes it.

17.

In which Sylvester appears to have created the first trans-Atlantic butterfly rescue and conveyance system. He is mistaken.

18.

In which the hat clerk discovers the rejuvenating properties of bark harvested during a full moon from an as-yet unclassified wetlands shrub located in the marsh through which Janice jogs. Both the marsh and the plot thicken.

19.

Herein the notorious "vampire" chapter, in which Sylvester is bitten by a rabid bat and wanders the moors carrying the moon on a stick before realizing he has only been bitten by a spider in his sleep. This chapter, by all extant evidence, seems to have at various points of development been absent from the documentary evidence concerning the frequent outlining of this fascinatingly unwritten novel, suggesting a great deal of vision and revision attendant upon the planning for its eventual inclusion. The page and chapter numbering in recently uncovered later versions supports the conjectures among several previous critics that the rumors of its inclusion were indeed true, despite what some critics have suggested about the chapter's potentially contrary tone.

20.

Inexorably, Sylvester begins his decline into madness. Tragically, critics of the Determinist School would have it, his tortured fall does not appear to be the fault of the spider bite.

21.

Pausing to observe an unusual butterfly perched on the head of a patient bullfrog, Janice is approached from behind by an awkward mangy-haired brute, who succeeds in subduing her only to experience humiliation at his inability to determine what it is he should do next. Janice presses her temporary advantage and escapes despite an annoying pebble in her running shoe. The attacker is quickly captured and returned to the asylum.

22.

In which the second corpse appears, thickening in the bog near the grove of medicinal bark trees. Darkness has engulfed the twilight frenzy of feeding bats. An opossum pauses to nose the pocket of the corpse's muddy pants but loses interest.

23.

In which a mournful Appalachian folk song is heard drifting on the wind across the meadow, accompanied by the clawhammer plunk of a homemade banjo. The words are lost on the wind, but clearly, it's a lament.

24.

Sylvester wandering the marsh at night. Is it today? Yesterday? The day before? The assault of decay from the muck that rises with each step no longer affects him. His white hat hangs by its chin strap behind his head, streaked green and black with swamp grass and bog muck. From time to time he just sits and watches his legs, eyeing them slowly down from his naked waist to his lolling manhood to the surface of the oily swamp water and on into the oblivion of the teeming darkness beneath. His pale skin and blonde body hair catch the moon's full light where he brushes his hand to ease the itch of insect bites.

25.

A basket of bark-stripped branches resting on the jogging path. Eight folded pages of carefully organized description of the patterns, colors and relationships of the freshly revealed surfaces. The wind lifts the pages as if trying to read them, but the naked branches close them again each time. No one appears to claim the basket.

26.

A habit of mist emerging. Quietly placed in previous scenes, it's thicker and more frequent now. And here a whole chapter devoted to the wet increase of weather.

27.

A body floating past the jogging path, its shape barely showing, submerged and softly bobbing. No, it's a log lifted from its grave by the slowly rising water. A few minutes later a white hat.

28.

In which the corpses multiply, animal and human alike, floating upon the
current, which moves now over the top of the jogging path. Morning melds
into day in a long gray pall. Night seems to have softened. The edges are gone.

29.

In which the flies are mating once more, hitchhikers islanded on a wet pale
compass of flesh.

30.

In which the bodies have caught on tree limbs and bridge pilings,
squirming with larvae, farting gas pockets and sluffing loose skin. On the
muddy bridge a man in a yellow slicker speaks of "investigations" and "claims"
and gestures to another man running a crane mounted on double truck wheels.
His exhausting patience is detailed. An ambulance approaches so slowly
you can hear the wet pull of the mud on the road as it clings then falls away
from the wheels. Slowly the details add up. The man in the slicker, we must
conclude, is Sylvester. But what of his madness?

31.

In which nature is recovering from its own devastation, without the aid of
biblical intervention. Each plant, each lucky animal adjusting and going on.
Already the dried mud is dusting away in the hot sun. Herons fattening in
the pools of cutoff water where fish have been trapped. Robins so heavy with
worms they look as if they couldn't fly. Buds popping open everywhere.

32.

In which Janice can be seen jogging from a long way off as the dried mud
dusts up into the hot still air. Suggestions of dime store Western redemption
playfully tossed off and discarded. Janice, then, closer up, suffering in the heat
as she continues down the trail that looks like it will never end.

33.

In which evening arrives with an abundance of mosquitoes and small
darting creatures thickening the air in swirling patterns of movement that
makes it look like the water, which has fully receded, is still there. Small birds

dart in and out of the long streams of insects, parting and reforming like waving handkerchiefs and insect ropes tugging at the light in the fading sky. Finally the creatures settle, full-bellied, onto the budding branches, and the bats take their place.

Afterword
In which the effect of various types of framing devices upon the painting is considered.

A DELIVERY

THE OAK DOOR opened, and a hand reached out and plucked the small package from its roost on top of the mailbox.

Two men heard the body hit the ground. Neither of them noticed the woman behind the stained-glass door following her shadow into the next room.

And if it were not for the old woman with the glass eye, the police would have found him. He was not himself, of course, but someone else might have been fooled.

The mirror clouded, and the visitor turned away, trying hard not to hear the chink of bricks falling into place in the hallway of the underground chamber. The scream echoed down the damp corridor and faded into the scurry of small feet and the dripping of water.

He began laughing, and his throat tightened. He listened to his heartbeat. It grew heavy. The wind scattered leaves across the empty porch. He reached for his hat, and a flutter of dust and wings rose from the closet shelf.

HOW I DIED IN THE WAR

IN THE BOOK of dreams there is a story about how you successfully avoided getting involved in local politics. The book of dreams is a book about looking for something in a place stories come to when they escape. Since no one has ever read all of it, we have nothing but each other's words to tell us that any of our stories are living there. When I read your story about local politics, I thought it was my story about how I died in the war. That's why I think your story is living in the book of dreams.

One thing I like about your story is how it seems to be about picking up the pieces, the way you go around finding where your legs and hands and mouth are and then the way you find your story coming out of the mouths of gamblers and falling into . . . but I don't want to tell your story for you.

How about "The Rowboat" as a title for your story?

When he came to the grave of his legs, he watched an old man looking under boulders for moanings. "Shoulda least seen 'em by now," the old man muttered. "Little buggers never was 'at sneaky afore." He gave the old man the nighthawk he had slung over his shoulder. The old man stroked the fur on its belly and started purring. "Damned if I unnerstan' it," the old man said softly, "but they's scared ta death a these moanin's. Even the dead uns."

In the tavern there was talk of the election. The Chief of Pots' wife had decided to run for Stickmaster. A badger hobbled in and sent the bartender into the back for the Captain of Snails. One of his men was slumped in the corner, peering out from under a blanket of headaches, quietly dumping the silence out of the empty jugs of noise. The badger gave the Captain of Snails a description of the three highwaymen who had beaten and robbed him. They could have been almost anyone.

When he came to the grave of his hands, he sat on a stone and began writing down all that had happened. He could see the old man walking between the stones and the dead trees with the nighthawk tied to his arm, holding it out in front of him and giggling. Sometimes the old man would stop and stroke the nighthawk's fur and mutter softly. Then he would hold it out in front of him and giggle again.

He came to another tavern, and there was a dung beetle, a scorpion, and a large sand crab. They were fighting over a ball of dung that had been sprayed with something by the bartender. Large amounts of money were at stake. The arena was a small rowboat half-filled with sand. Twigs and stones and pieces of glass were stuck in the sand like obstacles in a maze.

When he came to the grave of his mouth the story roared and rose over his head into the mouths of gamblers. What it was saying made his limbs feel stiff and hollow. One of his legs cracked, and as he turned, something hot sliced into the opening at his knee, jamming into the torn cartilage. He shivered and felt dizzy. He thought of a body floating on a low roll of waves in a bay. He climbed into a small rowboat and began rowing. He could hear the shuffle of money changing hands, and as he got closer, he could see a second body floating next to the first.

The badger scowled at the Captain of Snails. The Captain of Snails poured another vodka and lime. "I don't know how you see it, but I see it as two cutthroats that got their throats cut."

When he came to the grave of his story, the old man was waiting with the nighthawk. Moanings were coming out from under the boulders, making soft low rumbling noises that threatened to gather into something larger. The old man handed him the nighthawk. He giggled and watched the dung beetle rolling away the prize.

Another thing I like about your story is how it doesn't make excuses. My story about how I died in the war was like that.

Another thing I like about your story is the way it ends.

UNNATURAL ATTRACTIONS

A WOODEN BATHTUB, feeling its attraction for an old woman taking a bath, made little waves in the hot water. It frightened the old woman, but it made her wrinkled skin quiver, and it had been a long time since she had been quivered, so she just held herself there in the bathtub and let herself be taken advantage of.

A mouse crawled up onto the edge of the bathtub and watched the old woman, thinking now she is dying maybe there will be some scraps for me.

But the bathtub grew cold, and the old woman grew even more wrinkled, and the mouse fell in the water and drowned, and the water went singing on its way to the river where lots of little fishes were quivering and becoming big fishes.

GIFTS OF SILVER FISH

EVENING APPROACHES. Fog moves in from the ocean. One wheel at a time, an old woman lifts her cartload of fish up onto the wooden planks of the pier. The fishing boats bob, and the soft slap of waves rolling in from the mouth of the cove brush faintly against the cliffs, mixing with the echoing thump of wooden wheels like the sound of a child dragging a heavy stick against a fence as she moves in the fog down the long pier.

Slowly the fog clears, and the moon appears, a distant lighthouse, its reflection bobbing in the water. The old woman tips her cartload of fish into the light and watches their silver scales flash as they swim down into the darkness. Tomorrow the men will return. Their boats will be full of fish.

The village sits at the edge of a small inlet as if it were just crawling out of the water. Wolves sleep in the caves above the village. At night they come down to the docks in search of fish scraps. On the nights following a good catch, they are led by a white wolf that lives with an old woman in the hills. If enough scraps are not left to feed the wolves, the fishing turns bad.

Three women walk on the beach in the early morning, talking about how things begin. They talk about the legends of their village. They are young. They imagine stories that would explain things. They try to remember as far back as they can. What is it like to be born? On other days they will want to know about love.

One of the women is fat. She knows of a story she is afraid to tell the other two women. She thinks they would laugh. She thinks they would say that she made it up because she is fat. But often, when she is walking on the beach or lying in her bed at night, she remembers the story of the stone tree.

During the time of the stone tree, the sky had come down to the earth many times and many mysterious children had been born to them, and strange things had happened to these children, and they had died, and again there was nothing for a long time. Except the fat pit. And the stone tree standing beside it. For a long time that was all.

Then the wind came, and it blew hard against the stone tree, so hard that it stirred up the fat at the top of the fat pit. And with the first rough swell, two very large lumps of fat broke loose and rolled like jelly over the surface of the fat pit until the wind had given them so much momentum that they rolled right out onto the earth beneath the stone tree. And the lumps of fat began changing shape. One of them was very large and round, and the other one almost came apart when it rolled under the stone tree. Now it had two faces and a very thin body, almost as if each of the faces were trying to take something away from the body.

And as these two stood there, some new smaller lumps came rolling out of the fat pit. But each of these new lumps had something wrong with it. One of them was very tall and thin and had one leg shorter than the other, and it was off balance so that it leaned back away from the longer leg, which was always sticking out. And one of them was very small like a midget, except for the left hand, which was very large and looked as if it were badly swollen.

And there was a lump with gray hair, which had formed more perfectly than any of the others but had started getting old and was already wrinkled and dying. The midget with the big left hand carried it over to the fat pit and dropped it back in.

And there were two lumps who seemed to be twins with almost no arms or legs at all that had to sway from side to side in order to move.

By the time the midget had returned the dying lump to the fat pit, the wind had completely vanished, and there was nothing left for the remaining lumps to do but go off in search of their future.

Finally the fat woman tells her two friends the story of the stone tree. She tells them it is a legend her grandmother told her when she was a child. The two friends listen because the fat woman is their friend, but they believe she made it up. Or dreamed it because she is fat.

A few miles down the coast from the village, a rock wall rises from the shore. Gulls and large seabirds ride the air currents that rise from the water, straining to reach the top of the cliff where some of the villagers graze their sheep. Then it rises again to another plateau that stretches as far as you can see back into the hills.

Once a week the farmers come here with their crops to exchange them for fish, and each time they come, the fat woman hides. The farmers make her feel embarrassed because her friends tease her about the way the farmers talk about her. The farmers are friendly to her, and they talk about what it is like to make the land grow things with their animals and children growing and helping to keep the crops coming up. But it makes her feel as if they want her to be the mother of all that growing, and she begins to feel as if she is swelling up inside. The village boys tell her she is going to be a cornwife, and she runs away.

So now she hides on the cliff when the farmers are trading with the fishermen and watches the birds soar and the ocean reaching as far as she can see, and she feels better. And she wants never again to feel the world swell up inside of her.

One summer an old woman from the village begins to claim that she has the knowledge of the skies. She waits for a day when the fishermen have brought home many fish, and the wolves are sure to come down from the mountains. She hides herself in a blanket on the bottom of a small fishing boat and waits till she hears the wolves tearing at the fish scraps on the pier. Suddenly she jumps up from her hiding place, and the wolves stare, surprised. Another old woman in a white robe moves quietly down the pier and stands among the wolves as if they were old shepherds' dogs. The woman with the knowledge of the skies slowly raises her arms, glaring defiantly at the wolves. Rain begins falling. Softly at first, then stronger, the rain pours down. A streak of lightning crosses the sky, and one of the wolves whimpers. The woman in the white robe reaches out and gestures with her hand as if she were hurling a spear at the woman in the boat. Immediately, one of the wolves leaps. But a wave rocks the boat, and the wolf splashes into the water. The woman in the boat leans her head back in a laugh, rising above the noise of the rain. A second wolf leaps, locking his jaws around her exposed neck.

The next day the sun rises in a clear sky. The fishing boats sit idle along the pier, sails too limp to carry them. Fishermen play cards and throw dice on the decks, waiting for the wind. A few of the lighter boats try to row out of the harbor. Two of these manage to get far enough but return in the evening with no fish.

The wives of the fishermen mend nets by the long pier that reaches out a wooden arm to the water. The nets move up and down at the tears where their hands are moving in the coarse fibers. They seem to roll up and down with the waves as well as jerking with the quick motions of the mending needles. From the ocean we can see only the nets with their strange movements and the needles flashing as the sun peeks out from behind a cloud. From the shore, we would see the women. We would see them as the farmers see them, and the fishermen when they have docked their boats. But from the ocean we see only a mystery.

The fat girl dreams of mysteries. In one of them she is walking at night in the farmlands. She carries a lamp filled with whale oil, and she is thinking of the ship that must have brought the whale oil. She imagines the captain of the ship is a wide-eyed man with a gray speckled beard. He wears buckskin and breechcloth and orders his men around with sweeping gestures of his hands and a voice like a bellows.
The scene changes, and she stands beside a hole in the ground. Something thick and bubbling begins to fill the hole, and the wind begins blowing. Standing beside the hole in the moonshadow of a dead tree, she can imagine the captain pulling a small plow through the rocky ground, and this disappoints her.

The next evening a small boy watches from the roof of a boatshed as the wolves come down to the docks. As the wolves pass beneath the boatshed, the boy tosses fish down to them from a basket made of coarse reeds. On the hillside above the boatshed, an old woman stands quietly beneath a dead tree, watching.

While the wolves eat the fish, the boy wanders near the docks collecting plants for medicine and tea. On a hill above the docks, he finds a clutter of bones too big to be fish bones. He passes his hands through the dirt and uncovers a skull with hair still clinging to it. For a moment he is scared. Then he puts the bones on the plants in his basket and walks on toward the hills above the farmland.

One day the fat girl comes down to the docks before sunrise to watch the fishermen leaving. One of the men asks her if she would like to go along. She is shy and does not answer but gets on the boat when the man is not looking. When the fisherman sees her, he smiles.

All day long the fishing is very good, and the boats return riding low in the water, their holds heavy with fish. The girl watches as wagons and carts come down to meet the boats. But no one is driving them. And yet the animals stop at the docks as if they had been commanded to. It is the first time she has witnessed the wives of the fishermen coming to meet the fishermen at the docks from this side, from the ocean. She feels happy to be seeing the families sharing this secret and tries to remember which women belong to which carts and wagons, and what they will look like when she steps onto the shore, and she can see them again.

The fat girl works through the night cleaning fish for the man who took her out in his boat, and it is nearly dawn when she finally goes home. Her thoughts roll and toss like waves against the bow of her body's hunger. She gets out of bed to watch the sun rise and begins walking.

She is standing on a hill when she sees the boy, and she raises her arm to wave at him, but the boy does not see her. She follows the boy to ask what he is doing in the hills so early in the morning, thinking because of the basket that he is probably looking for berries. But the boy is walking fast, and she can't seem to catch up to him. The boy begins climbing up a steep hill, and the fat girl can see when he has gone into a cave part way up the hill. But by the time she can get to the cave, the boy is gone. She sees the basket farther back in the cave and goes to see what is in it. She picks up the bones and looks at them. Suddenly she is very tired.

When the girl wakes up, the cave is filled with dogs. At least that is what
the girl thinks as she is waking up. Gradually, as sleep leaves her farther and
farther behind, she realizes they are not dogs but wolves. Still, they act like
dogs, and one of them is lying beside her. Another is sleeping next to the basket
of bones, as if it were guarding them. A wolf with white fur comes into the
cave from the bright morning sunlight, and she wonders if she has slept only a
very short while or more than a day as the white wolf drops a large fish on the
floor of the cave.

The fish is nearly cooked, and the cool evening has just darkened into night
when the boy appears at the mouth of the cave. One of the wolves growls deep
in his throat, and the fat woman brushes her hand along the side of his neck
to quiet him. She offers the boy part of the fish and wonders if the boy is just
quiet or if he cannot speak.

It is still dark when the girl hears a noise like a cough. She quickly rises
and moves instinctively towards the fire. An old woman watches her from the
darkness at the back of the cave. The boy sits up and stares. For a moment
none of them move. And then the old woman steps forward into the light and
removes two strips of dried meat from beneath her robe and offers them.

Evening approaches. Fog moves in from the ocean. One wheel at a time, an
old fat woman lifts her cartload of fish up onto the wooden planks of the pier.

On the hill above the docks an old bearded man is carrying a basket made
of coarse reeds. He is looking for plants to make medicine and tea. Some of the
medicines are for dreams. Some of the dreams are for the old woman.

The moon's reflection bobs in the water by the dock. The woman tips her
cartload of fish into the light and watches their silver scales flash as they swim
down into the darkness. Out of the darkness swims the moon. Out of the
patterns of their lives the fishermen build dreams. Each one different. Each
one an explanation for something that has already happened and may happen
again. Each one a lifetime. Each one flashing briefly in the moonlight, a silver
fish shaking the hook.

NEAR THE CHURCH AT CORTOVINA

WE HAVE BEEN waiting a long time. An old man scrambles over a mound of rocks carrying an oysterbasket on the hill where Tatovia lies. Two boys swirl out a net from a small boat in the bay. Up on the hill a woman stands in the vineyard staring down on the white stucco houses with their red tiled roofs. I have nothing to tell you that will not happen without me.

Twilight slips through blue stained glass, a shaft of dusty light on an empty urn. Behind the church brown clubs burst into ragged fur, molting like seasoned animals. A reed unfolds wings, hauls itself up into the sky dragging two yellow sticks of marsh-grass for legs. A guinea hen struts by the hayrack. Tarred boats bob and bump against the dock. Think of all that could have happened. We have been waiting a long time.

Stones like tiny platforms left behind at low tide. Fingerpools. Nothing so simple it cannot help us. But when it finally comes, we have nothing to say. We walk to the ocean through snow.

EYE OF THE BEAST

1.

IN THE EARLY morning, smoke rises from the Lautreau farm near the
village of Parlaute in the south of France. It is near harvest and burning
anything at this time is unusual.

The smoke rises slowly in the still morning. The Lautreau farm is quiet.
At the other farms chores are being attended to. A young goat jumps
into the air and lands again in the same spot. A farm wife looks up from
milking and wonders, again, what the Lautreaus could be burning. If there
were any sign of an uncontrolled fire, she would immediately go to help,
but the smoke is soft and billowy like the smoke of a smoldering pile of
dried manure.

From the road in front of the Lautreau farmhouse, the smell of the
smoke is unpleasant. Beside the side road leading past the farmhouse to the
outbuildings arranged in a horseshoe shape, open end facing the fields, there
is an old wooden barrel containing cornsilk which has discolored to browns
and blacks. The dew gives it a soggy thickness. From here it is evident that
the smoke is coming from the center of the horseshoe of buildings. From the
edge of the horseshoe, it is impossible to mistake the odor.

When the small pile of smoldering bodies forces one to turn away, one might suddenly think again about the cornsilk, or notice the ears strung on wire between two of the buildings, poised there like a family of morning doves.

Jean, Jacques and Pierre pull their rickety cart down a deserted country lane bordered by broad fields of wind-stirred wheat. Early morning stillness has been replaced by a gradual invasion of southern winds. The young men's blouses and pantaloons flap in the breeze. The tassel on the end of Jacques' stocking cap bounces against his back as the wind catches it. The cart creaks and bumps as the young men playfully take turns pulling it.

They cross a cobblestone bridge and their load jiggles in the hay. One of the heads begins rolling off the cart, but Jacques catches it before it can fall to the cobbles. He carries it to the ledge of the bridge and holds it over the water as if to tempt whatever lurks there. Hearty laughter erupts from all three of them. Jacques yells at the others. They begin tossing it and singing. Soon they have three heads flying about in the air between them, then four, then five. But they quickly tire of the game and one by one put the heads back in the cart. As they relay the last one to Jacques, who is closest to the cart, he pulls a dagger from the top of his pantaloons, and in one smooth motion thunks it into the last pale head. An eye pops from it like a large seed as the dagger skewers it. Jacques picks it up and hides it under his eye-patch. The others laugh but seem anxious now to be on their way. Jacques lifts the eye-patch and catches the eye as it rolls down his cheek. He crosses his heart and throws it over his shoulder.

Paulette is on her way to visit Uncle Lautreau. This is the first time she has been allowed to go alone, even though the Lautreau farm is less than two miles away. Soon she will come to the main road. From there it's half a mile to the cobblestone bridge and another half a mile to Uncle Lautreau's farm. It's a cool still morning, and Paulette begins whistling. By the time she reaches the bridge, she has worked up enough courage to gaze over the ledge in defiance of the stories she has been told. She convinces herself that the stories, after all, are not that frightening, and she begins pulling at the cobblestones in search of loose ones to throw in the water. Suddenly she sees the eye and stares at it. She tries to convince herself it came from someone's fish dinner. She hurries on to tell Uncle Lautreau what she has seen.

Dartemont sits by the cracked window of his small house waiting for the return of his three sons. Since the death of his wife, he has been patiently

waiting. The house has been purged of the supernatural. Even the horseshoe
over the door has been removed, and there is a lighter shade of wood there
where for so long the weather could not so easily reach that part of the house.

Paulette reaches into the barrel of cornsilk and grabs a handful. She runs to
the farmhouse to ask Uncle Lautreau why he is saving it and would he please,
oh please, use it to fix her dolly's head that lost all its hair. But there is no one
in the farmhouse. They must be where the smoke is.

As she reaches the edge of the horseshoe of farm buildings, she
understands that something is wrong; the smell, the horrible smell, and
where are Uncle Lautreau and the others? Confused and growing more
and more terrified as she runs for home, coming closer and closer to the
cobblestone bridge, where the eye will be staring at her, she clutches tightly,
without thinking, her handful of cornsilk.

Dartemont dreaming is Dartemont possessed, possessed by visions of his
wife's last hours, after they accused her and took her away. He wants to believe
that she was innocent, but he remembers now the strange shape of the scar he
had thought nothing of, nestled on her inside thigh.

Paulette crosses the bridge without looking down, and growing more
confused as she nears home, tries to think of what to say. By the time she finds
her mother behind the house, her thoughts are so jumbled she can't speak.
Her mother waits patiently, knowing because she is out of breath that she has
something important to say.

Suddenly noticing the cornsilk she has been clutching, Paulette thrusts it
out in front of her and smiles because she has thought of something to say. "It
feels like hair." Her mother rubs it between her fingers and nods, confusion and
curiosity surfacing in her expression. Then, just as suddenly, Paulette's smile
breaks, and she begins sobbing and choking out confused bits of her story.

2.

Early spring. Paulette's story is changing. The water in the pond is cold,
and it gives her goose bumps. Her breasts roll a little as she splashes, and she

laughs like she used to when Uncle Lautreau would bounce her on his knee and make noises like a galloping horse.

The day is warm and still, but the spring weather has not yet had time to have much of an effect on the temperature of the pond, and Paulette stays in the water only a few minutes before she begins shivering. She is dressed and drying her hair when Jean's voice startles her.

"You're shivering. It's not warm enough for swimming yet."

Paulette, drying her hair, shivering, says nothing.

"Why do you ignore me? What have I done?"

"How long were you watching?"

Now it is Jean's turn to say nothing. He kicks at a dirt clod and smiles in a way that he intends to mean that because he is in love with her, there is nothing wrong. Paulette, unconvinced, waits for an answer. Jean does not allow the silence to remain long.

"I came to tell you that your mother has accepted an invitation to dinner with my family tomorrow. I was hoping you would come with her."

"I don't like your family."

"Do you like me?"

"I don't trust you."

"You think I am too old for you."

"That too."

The silence returns and Jean stumbles for something to say. "My brothers and I will be rich soon."

Dartemont peering from a pile of woolen blankets stares at the door, expecting Jacques and Pierre to be returning with his medicine. They have been gone a long time. His own sons do not recognize the seriousness of his illness. But he will say nothing because the last time he began babbling and dreamed of his wife for days. However wicked they seem, he will never again call them devils.

And what of Jean? Jean who is better than the others? He is off building something for that Lautreau girl, as if he no longer cared for his father.

Jean and Paulette walk without speaking. Paulette shivers as they cross the cobblestone bridge. Jean slides his arm around her waist and draws her closer to him. She does not resist.

Jacques and Pierre stumble through the door, obviously drunk, carrying
half a dozen bottles between them, two of them empty. Pierre stops suddenly,
and putting his hands on Jacques' shoulders, steadies himself. Gazing into
Jacques' face with as serious an expression as he can muster, he slowly raises
his right hand and covers one eye. Then he slowly raises his left hand, flicks his
nose with his thumb, and winks. Now Jacques slowly raises his right hand and
covers his good eye, then slowly raising his left hand he suddenly flicks his nose
with his thumb and begins laughing. Dartemont watches without smiling.

Jacques uncorks a new bottle, takes a drink, and tosses it to him. It lands
on Dartemont's blankets with a soft gurgle, nearly upright. Jacques laughs.
Dartemont grumbles.

Jean slides his hand along Paulette's side, brushing against her breast as he
moves it to the back of her neck and back down around her waist.

The sound of the saw moves down the small valley into the sparse trees and
climbs the hills on both sides of the stream. The water curves around the small
peninsula on which Jean is working. Already the four square walls are strong
and well anchored in the hard earth beneath them.

3.

An old woman gazes out the window at him, but she does not see him.
One of the shutters sags from a broken hinge. A magpie in a wicker birdcage
hanging from the corner of the roof squawks and peers in the other direction.
The old woman's head moves in and out of the window as if she were expecting
someone.
The man peeing against the side of the rain barrel does not see him. The
cow tethered beside the barn does not see him. The small brown dog with the
studded collar who is snarling at a chicken does not see him. But he is there.

He is known for his staff with the bulbous knob on the end. How this
came about, since no one has seen him, is a matter for folklore. We have other
reasons for believing he is there. We have Jean's story.
As Jean builds the story he remembers a painting he saw once when he was

very young and the farm was prospering and his mother took him to Paris with her. Slowly, as he tries to make a story and Paulette's interest encourages him, he remembers details and adds to what he remembers.

The man is thin and has a long nose. He carries a pack with small animal furs hanging from it. He has a knife with fur on the handle. There is a small claw embedded in the fur. There is a soupspoon hanging from his pack and he wears a slipper and there is a rag tied around his leg where he hurt it and a crow is sitting in a dead tree and there is a hawk wheeling overhead are you listening?

"I'm sorry. What were you saying?"

"A hawk."

"No, about the man. Is he a vagabond?"

"Sort of."

"A highwayman?"

"That's not the next part of the story."

"What then?"

"A nuthatch."

"Why a nuthatch?"

"There are holes in the house."

"So?"

"The nuthatch lives in one of the holes."

"So why is that important?"

"That's not the next part of the story."

"What then?"

"Some children playing in the dust by the house."

"Why are they important?"

"Because they don't see the man either."

"I'm getting tired. Tell me the rest later."

For more than a week, Dartemont has been delirious. Because he and his sons have grown rich, more than one doctor has had to listen to his fevered plaints for forgiveness. He tells them he is sorry for not believing in her. He mutters about the scar. He tells them he was outnumbered. They were so sure. They told him there was a confession. They found teeth marks. Dartemont begins explaining things. He explains the weather. He explains the chickens that haven't been laying. He knows the reason for brown rocks. He knows why it is raining. He knows why it is not raining.

The last doctor thought he was demented. Jacques and Pierre nodded. A hard life. They say nothing about their mother.

"Jean? Jean, answer me."

"What?"

"Do you remember that story you were telling me?"

"No."

"Why couldn't anyone see the vagabond?"

"I can't remember."

"Was he evil?"

"Probably."

"I thought that's what it was going to be. Why didn't you just say that?"

"Then it wouldn't have been a story. Besides, I like the part about the fish."

"What fish? You never told me that part."

"Do you want to hear it?"

"Well, I guess so."

"The old woman is cooking them."

"Is the vagabond there?"

"Yes, but they can't see him."

"Who else is there?"

"The children and the man who was peeing against the rain barrel."

"Is he the husband?"

"No, the husband is dead. He just helps out because the old woman can't do everything, and he doesn't have anywhere else to go."

"How come? Is he a vagabond too?"

"Ah, yes. He is a vagabond too."

"No, that's too easy. He is a neighbor. He had a farm but he lost it and he doesn't have any family."

"Okay, but he's old and he has a hunched back and he can't do as much work as he's supposed to."

"Why does he have to be ugly?"

"Because it's a true story."

"Then I don't like true stories."

"Okay, then I won't tell you how it ends."

"I don't care how it ends."

"Jean? Jean, answer me."
"What?"
"When are you going to finish the house?"
"It's harvest. I don't have time."
"Maybe your brothers should do more work so you have time."
"Maybe."
"Where are your brothers?"
"I don't know."
"I knew they weren't helping you. Doesn't it make you angry?"
"I don't know."
"That's not a very good answer."

"Jean, what if we were in a story?"
"What?"
"You know. What if somebody made us up?"
"Then we wouldn't have much to say about it, would we?"
"No, I guess not."

4.

Paulette's story is dreaming. It has a beast in its dreams. The beast won't go away until Jean finishes the cabin and Jean will never finish the cabin because Jean is bored with that story. In one of the dreams the beast has two heads. The two heads have three eyes.

"Jean, Jean don't let him hurt me," says her voice in the dream. The two heads turn towards each other, smile and . . .

On the hill outside the cabin the beast is moving. Paulette dreams. In her dream the beast changes its shape as soon as she imagines it clearly. She is afraid, but she is curious. She wants to see what it is that she is afraid of. But the beast keeps changing its shape, as if whatever she imagined the beast was, it was, but now it is something else.

On the hill outside the cabin, the eye rolls anxiously back and forth.

When Pierre is the beast, he is making love to her, and then he is stuffing her with eyes. He pulls them out of his penis with a soft pop and stuffs them

into her and she hates him and she is excited and she cannot help watching
Jacques who is popping them into his mouth and cracking them like chestnuts
as he watches Pierre make love to her.

When Jacques is the beast, he is wearing his black eye-patch over the wrong
eye, and he can see things deep inside of her that belong to him. And it is Jean
who has undressed her.

At first Paulette was very frightened by the dreams, but now most of them
are the same, and it is like living in an old house with rotten floors and bugs
and broken windows and it is not a good place but it is much worse when you
first live there than when it has become most of what you know.

Like most old houses, this one has a secret room. Paulette has been in the room
many times, but she can never remember what is in there. Sometimes she thinks it
is the beast, sometimes only the beast's eye. Sometimes she thinks it is Jean.

The sound of the saw moves down the small valley into the sparse trees and
climbs the hills on both sides of the stream. The water curves around the small
peninsula on which Jean is working. On the top of a hill overlooking the valley
that shelters the unfinished cabin there is a soft round jelly of viscous white
with a black hole in the center. In the hole are all the dreams of the people it
has seen. That is why it is telling a true story.

5.

In the early morning breeze the smoke curls and billows up from the
charred timbers of the burnt cabin. The stream curls around the peninsula and
another small lump of earth falls from its neck. A dark cloud whirls out into the
stream. Soon the cabin's blackened remains will be the center of an island.

Jean pulls his rickety cart over the cobblestone bridge and begins laughing
uncontrollably. Even the three heads seem oddly humorous as he rolls, giggling,
in the grass by the side of the bridge. Suddenly he stops laughing, folds his legs
underneath him, and sits at the side of the road, staring deep into the eyes of the
three heads, lingering over Paulette's. Then he jumps up with his dagger in his
hand, pops the eyes out of all three heads, and strews them over the cobblestones.

NEAR TORSHAVN, FARÖE ISLANDS

WALKING IN THE WIND my clothes billow and I wave as if from
the deck of a returning ship. Far below, fishing boats move slowly to deeper
water. On the cliffs between us, puffin-hunters scramble and shout. Something
in my life has swollen. My emotions strain to contain it. Daylight swallows
the moon. Peninsulas, split like stone fingers from my country's hand, hold a
watery gleam, deceptive as love, in the web of their fingers. This land feeds its
gradual loss into the cold bright water. Summer leaves as though it were one of
us, awash with emotion. The long darkness waits, despair holding off the coast
in quiet boats.

An early morning squall chases over the islands and small villages hidden
in the sheltered bays. Wet cliffs sparkle in the emerging sunlight, seabirds
weaving and calling over the rocks. I remember the long bright nights of
summer, darkness fallen away in the middle of dreams. I sat on the porch in
the constant light and remembered spring when everything was shouting.
Could I have been unhappy?

Again I have come back from the long passage we repeat in the heart. I
row my boat past the mill. Mayflies and moths dart about in the shadows. A
caterpillar plops into the water, and I can almost feel the trout's excitement in
my stomach. A swarm of soft, cool wings covers me. I look up and wave my
arms as if that might hold my place.

THE BLACK SWAN

FOR MANY YEARS Seju and his family had lived in Samoki-by-the-Sea, and often Seju felt it was an exciting place to live. There was a certain caution enemies held in their eyes when they discovered you lived in Samoki-by-the-Sea, and Seju looked forward to the day when he would be old enough to drink with the poets and gamblers and make love with the women. Already Seju knew how to talk like a long lost friend with the men of the village, and the names of their favorite women rolled off his young tongue like a litany of sins devoutly to be wished for.

But in Seju's family there was great respect for the lives and customs of the people of Samoki-by-the-Mountains, for it was there that wealth and honor were to be found. And it was there that people believed in magic and noble blood. And it was to Samoki-of-the-Mountains that all but the most stubborn or hopeless turned their thoughts and dreams in the season of ceremonies, for it was in the season of ceremonies that the true social order of Samoki was established, altered, and re-established. If any resident of either village desired a change in social position, it was the season of ceremonies that gave them their chance.

In the mountains, changes were taking place; the setting out of the finest sweetmeats at the baker's, the appearance of finer quality silks at the tailor's, the gradual shifting from bone remedies and ointments for the cure of skin disease to love potions and exotic aromas for the breath and body at the apothecary's.

Suddenly the houses were filled with motion. The last of the summer's dust flew in small clouds from the windows and doors, and all the servants walked around with red knees from scrubbing the floors. Rickshaw drivers became suddenly prosperous and strong from carrying wealthy patrons up and down the hill. A final flurry of boats arrived in the harbor carrying the last of the rich back from long summer holidays and seasonal homes in the islands.

In the midst of all this budding change, Seju continued to fish with the old fisherman called Blue, listening carefully to his friends as the fish grew scarcer and their knowledge grew more and more valuable and waiting with careful attention for the signs of the last big migrations that would enter the waters nearby. And at night, tired and smelly, Seju walked quickly home to bathe and change clothes and return to the tables stained with beer, blood, and sometimes sex, where the emotions of Samoki-by-the-Sea's most durable citizens spilled over each evening and often far into the night.

The first of the seasonal ceremonies came and went with little notice by this social center of Samoki-by-the-Sea, and the second was well under way before an occasional comment began to fall on the tables among the dice, the beer, and the money. And it wasn't until the Ceremony of the Black Swan approached that any excitement out of the ordinary became apparent. Still, Seju returned home late from the company of his friends the poets and gamblers and arrived early with his friends the fishermen to test the sea again as it has been tested before and proven fruitful. It began to seem to Seju as if by simply ignoring the festivities of Samoki-of-the-Mountains he could go on forever with his happiness and the sea would bring him food and his friends would enliven his spirit.

But Seju's friends were growing dull and irritable, pounding on the tables and sometimes, more earnestly than before, on their friends, as if the growing excitement of Samoki-of-the-Mountains were taking place at their expense. And it was at this time of the year, as well, that the offshore winds moved in close to the harbor and slammed gigantic walls of water against the cliffs not far from the village, leaving a mist, and sometimes fog, hanging heavy in the air. There was not a fisherman among them, even drunk, foolish enough to go out against those winds.

Not far up the hill from the harbor, on the very edge of Samoki-by-the-Sea, lived a young girl and her mother. The girl's name was Ara. Her father, whose bald shiny head was the single most distinctive feature Ara could remember among a haze of scattered visits, was a politician. Beyond that, Ara was able to retrieve only scattered bits and pieces of information from the occasional lapses of her mother who habitually avoided any discussions of her father. Ara had accepted long ago, as her mother apparently had not, the fact that her father's political career had been, as they say, "spotted," not totally devoid of incriminating self-interest. But just exactly what those failings had amounted to, Ara was never able to discover, even as she grew older and became clever at tricking her mother into revealing things.

Some mornings, when Ara's mother had managed to rise early and attend to her baking, she would send Ara with a loaf of bread to Blue, the old fisherman who lived in a shack near where the fishermen cleaned their fish. When Ara was younger, she had once been sent to the old man's shack very early in the morning, and she had gone in without knocking. The old man was sitting at a desk, writing, wearing a red kimono that was open in the front. She stared at the old man's body, and because he was not embarrassed, she was glad that she could see it.

At first Ara had bothered her mother very often with questions about the old man's name, but in time it came to seem as if it were just exactly the right name for him, and it no longer mattered how he had gotten it. It did matter though that he was very mysterious about answering her questions when she stayed to talk with him. He would serve her tea, a different kind every time. And he would answer her questions with words that somehow seemed right but were always different and always more difficult than she thought they would be. Even when it was a very simple question. It was like that when she asked him what it was like to be old.

Ara liked him because he was honest but never ashamed when they talked and Ara asked him something he did not know. Often they would sit and wonder and make up stories to explain something they did not understand, and each story would be better than the last until they decided they had explained it.

It seemed to Ara as the time passed that the old man was beginning to avoid some of her questions about the season of ceremonies, but she was never quite sure, and she could find no reason why he might not want to answer questions about something she thought nearly everyone knew about.

For Ara it added up to curiosity, and she often went home dreaming of fantastic celebrations and puzzling over the answers that seemed confusing to her with a vision of the old man smiling and nodding as he had a way of doing whenever he answered one of her questions.

The windows above Ara's bed opened out on the small harbor where all summer long the boats had brought life to the summer village. One night Ara slipped from her bedclothes and went to the window to look out on the harbor. Seagulls floated on the warm air, and the quiet water hardly even bobbed a single fishing boat against the long pier. Ara looked down at her body and wished again, as she had in the winter, when the cold air made her shiver with goosebumps and her breath made clouds, that her breasts would grow bigger. She touched the nipples and thought of how the cold air would make them peek out like tiny animals.

Then she went to the closet by her bed and took the robe with the cranes on it and slipped it onto her shoulders. The smooth silk felt cool against her skin. She stood by the window and touched herself, carefully, as if she were blind.

Seju woke early, as he always did, dressed quickly, and walked to the docks. As always, the docks were full of busy fishermen, but this time they were mending nets, dry-docking boats, securing moorings and preparing their boats and their lives for the coming season of storms and the colder weather that would follow. You could not tell from the warm sun shining down on them and the sweat glistening from the bodies that anything was different today, but to Seju, who knew the motions of setting sail as well as he had ever known anything, it was painfully obvious that the fishing season was ending.

Even so, he went to the old man's hut, but no one was there. Seju turned and walked back up the path to his own house, but when he got there, it suddenly felt strange and foreign, and he continued walking up the hill. Two women came up the path with large bundles on their backs, and Seju asked them what they were carrying, but they only giggled and walked faster. Seju kept on walking and he looked at the different kinds of birds along the path as the path got higher, but they did not seem to mean anything to him.

He could feel by the way the sun felt on his shoulders that it was getting late, and yet he did not want to go home. He came to a fork in the path and took the path to the right for no particular reason. After a while there were stones in the path, long flat stones that must have been put there on purpose. As he walked further, the stones were closer together, and the path grew steeper. And then there was a wooden railing, and the bushes were all very neat. Some of them were trimmed to make patterns. Seju thought that it was almost as if he were walking up a long green stairway and pretty soon there would be a room. But the stairway seemed to go on forever, and Seju remembered that one of the men he knew who had lost a lot of money gambling had said that there were places in Samoki-of-the-Mountains where the streets were like a beautiful green maze.

The path turned to the right and then cut quickly back to the left again, and there, hidden in among the trees, was a house, the biggest house Seju had ever seen. And it seemed as if the house, too, were living. It seemed to grow out of the hillside, just like the trees.

Seju walked to the door and then realized he had no reason to be here, except for his desire to look, and he walked away from the door, around the corner of the house.

From that side Seju could see down into a courtyard that seemed to wander aimlessly between the walls of the house. There were walls with no roof over them as if the courtyard was intended to be divided into outdoor rooms. One of the walls stood in a small pond, dividing it in half. On one side was an elaborately carved wooden bench rising out of the water. Water plants hung on the water like a heavy green cloak spilling out onto the stones set into the earth that made the walkway. On the other side of the wall there were stone statues of naked people twined about each other. One of the statues was off to the side, a smoothly-carved, seated woman with her lap hollowed out. Her lap was filled with water, and a green towel was draped over her upraised arm.

Everywhere there were patterns of cane and reeds built into the walls. Many of them were water landscapes. Shorelines with tall thin birds. Swans swimming under bridges. Cranes flying into the sunset. Most of the scenes were done in different shades of cane and wood, but some of them had sharply detailed places of color. Especially deep red and a shiny black.

Seju walked down into the courtyard on a series of smooth black stones and looked into the rooms in the courtyard. The floors were covered with reed mats, and many of the rooms had more than one level to the floor. Most of the walls were no more than wooden frames with white paper or cloth on them, but a few were thick, solid, dark-grained wood. On some of the walls that could be seen farther into the house, scenes were painted like the ones in the courtyard, but with colors that seemed to change from room to room.

One of the rooms was very large with a great high ceiling. Huge round beams ran across the ceiling and they were twisted in the manner of trees that have grown too close to the ocean. It made Seju think of how hidden the house seemed to be among the trees on the hillside.

Along one wall of the room there was a long row of tall black chests with golden hinges and clasps. On top of the chests were large vases, tall and thin with colorful drawings on them. Above these was a row of hanging metal lanterns with latticework designs that made them look very delicate.

In the center of the room was a large circular fireplace and Seju could see ropes climbing along the nearest wall to the ceiling that must have been for controlling the panels recessed back from the rest of the ceiling that could open for the smoke from the fire. Chains hung down from the sides of the opening to a black stone shelf that hung about six feet above the fire. On the stone shelf was a large stone statue of a swan. In the fading light the swan seemed to have a dark blue tint.

Seju thought he heard a noise and turned quickly. In the far recesses of the room he could see a heavy wooden wall made of large slats of wood and reinforced with metal. Over the wall hung a large intricately carved sword.

Suddenly Seju realized that if he were found here he would be taken for a thief, and he quickly left the room and began the long descent down the mountain as the last light slipped away, the moon lighting his way among the shadows.

In Ara's dream she was wearing her robe, and the cranes were flying or standing in the water with their beaks stabbing at small fish. As the cranes grew more active, the robe lengthened. Ara rose above the village with her robe billowing out behind her, and the winds carried her out to sea. She came to a small fishing boat with a swan painted on the bow, and there in the water beside the boat a young woman was floating with a robe trailing off behind her into the water farther than Ara could see. The boat looked empty. The woman seemed to be sleeping, or dead, floating there in the water beside the empty boat.

It was very cold the next morning. The old man was having a hard time moving. His bones were complaining. He did not go fishing every day like most of the fishermen, and he was regretting that he had told Seju he would go today. At least he would have a strong young man to help him.

He knew that the big runs were over. The most he could hope for would be a couple of brief smaller runs tangling in his nets or a larger fish still lingering where the huge runs of the last few weeks had been so plentiful. Many of the fishermen had already hung up their nets for the season, and as he struggled with the morning fire, he decided today would be his last day too. He could not help but wonder, with the cold so deep in his bones, if it was not also his last season.

They had been fishing for many hours with only a couple of small tuna to show for it when the old man spotted a large white piece of canvas in the water. As they moved toward it, small broken pieces of burnt wood floated around them in the water. Suddenly the surface of the water was churning with small fish trying to escape from the larger fish feeding beneath them. Seju and the old man quickly threw out the nets, and for the rest of the afternoon they followed the sporadic feeding of the fish. Near dark they again found themselves in the midst of many pieces of what must have been a shipwreck and decided to make one last cast of the nets as a gesture to their good luck in finding the shipwreck swarming with fish.

As they pulled in the nets, the old man thought to himself how lucky they were, and he almost forgot how strong the pain was in his muscles and all through his body. But the nets came back easily with only a small dogfish, then a piece of wood, then a glass bottle with nothing but air inside it. But one last heavy black mass in the corner of the net turned out to be an intricately sewn robe with hundreds of small golden cranes on it. There was nothing in any of the pockets. Seju was so taken by its beauty and intricate stitching that he convinced the old man that it should be his pay for this lucky day. He hung it on the mast to dry as the wind carried them home.

Ara woke suddenly with a shadow lingering from her dream. She recognized a large bird's golden wing, then let the dream pass, and putting on her robe, stepped to the window and stared up at the sky. For a moment she seemed mesmerized. No sound broke the stillness, and she remained motionless. Then a cricket began chirping, and she thought how warm it was tonight, and it was a sad thought because she remembered the cold winds that came after the last warm days of fall.

As Ara listened to the cricket, a feeling of excitement was growing in her. She thought how exciting it would be to go out in the streets and up to the houses on the hill where the servants were preparing even now in the darkness for the ceremonies that would begin tomorrow. And as she imagined doing this, she saw herself clothed only in the robe she was wearing, with her nakedness a daring secret she would share with no one.

Seju could not sleep, and he rose from his mat feeling uneasy. His thoughts returned to the robe hanging on the wall in the corner. He went to it and felt the damp cloth. He felt haunted by the robe and by what had happened. He could not steady his excitement. He went out into the streets and started climbing them to the paths he remembered so clearly that he felt as if he had been there a hundred times before, when in fact he had been there only once.

The moon had been growing each night, and he had enough light to see by. In the houses he passed he could hear soft rustlings, and from time to time a shadow flickered across a wall as a candle wavered or someone moved in the house. But most of the houses were quiet and dark, for it was well into the night, and no one met him as he climbed the narrowing paths that twisted up the mountainside. He came to a fork in the path where the bushes were neatly trimmed and a wooden railing had been mounted into the earth. He remembered the turn to the right and the sudden turn back to the left, and his heart quickened as he watched the candles flickering in the night breeze. As he came closer, he could see figures moving in the courtyard. Or were they only shadows?

Seju moved behind the bushes at the side of the house till he could see the courtyard more clearly and tried to control his breathing as he watched. Three musicians were sitting in the shadows playing softly on two string instruments and a set of wooden blocks unlike anything Seju had seen before. The sounds were faint and haunting, drifting quickly away into the evening, leaving Seju uncertain of what he had heard.

Three women sat in black robes with their heads bowed on fur rugs next to the pond, and from time to time they slowly raised their heads, tossing their hair back, and then slowly lowered them again as if to follow some climactic passage in the music. This went on for the longest time, and Seju felt as if he were being hypnotized until, leaning too far to the side, his foot slipped. He caught himself in the bushes, holding still, waiting to see if he had been noticed. The music continued as before, but Seju was too frightened, and he ran.

Ara held the bread close to her in the cold morning breeze, wanting it to stay warm for Blue. When she got there, he seemed especially pleased by the bread, and they talked away the cold until it was nearly lunchtime. Ara turned to go. He seemed reluctant to let her leave, something that had never happened before, though she knew he enjoyed their conversation as much as she did. He started talking about the Ceremony of the Black Swan, spilling out all his memories of each year's ceremony, farther and farther back, till he was a young boy seeing it for the first time. And the wonder of all the elaborate preparations was there again, in all his movements and words. She grew excited with him and happy for him. He explained how in the past a young woman was chosen during the ceremony to become the bride of the richest unmarried man of Samoki-of-the- Mountains. More than once blood had been spilled over a bad choice, but most years it was a great occasion for celebration, and the poorer the new bride had been before being chosen, the greater the celebration was.

Suddenly the old man turned to Ara and grew quiet. A sad slow voice explained to her as he held her hands in his that a few rich men still chose their brides this way, and that they had such power it could be very dangerous to refuse them. He was silent for a long time, and Ara's hands grew sweaty between his.

"It is my duty to ask that you attend the ceremony."

Two nights before the ceremony, a great storm fell on the villages. Water washed down from the sky in huge waves. The ocean was rolling and sending water pouring in over the docks. Everyone feared a tidal wave, but it did not come, and by the middle of the next day, the sun was again shining.

Ara's feelings had been in nearly as great a state of unrest as the weather, but with the sun's return, she felt as if an opportunity had been placed before her. Why should she not marry? She was of the right age. And if she was to marry, why not a wealthy man? She carried these pleasant thoughts with her through the afternoon and began preparing.

During the night Seju's family had cowered in their small house, hoping the storm would not grow large enough to bring a tidal wave. It had happened once before in Samoki-by-the-Sea. There were only a few elders who really remembered it, but all of the residents felt as if each storm that passed had been a vivid reminder of their vulnerability.

Seju passed the night trying to offer his family a feeling of safety that he himself could not believe in. Yet he was not afraid, just aware of how easily the whole village could be carried out to sea. He did not say anything to frighten his mother or sister, but he did feel they had all been negligent in not making a few minor repairs in the house, for the roof was leaking very badly, and one shutter had broken at the storm's first gasp. There would be quite a mess to clean up when the storm finally did subside.

It ended more quickly than Seju had expected. After surveying the damage, he left his mother and sister at work on the broken shutter. They were reluctant to let him go, but he insisted he had to see how the old fisherman had weathered the storm.

Seju worried about the old man, of course, but he was, after all, an expert sailor and no stranger to the ways of the weather. He would be repairing the leaks and bailing out his hut long before Seju arrived to help him.

But when Seju got there, the hut was strangely quiet. The sun had come out and was shining softly through the slats in the window shutters onto the objects floating on the floor's new pond. There was no sign of the old man.

Seju remembered clearly what the old man had said about death. He had decided; when his time came, he would put out to sea in a small boat and let the sea decide the time. Seju ran to the old man's fishing boat. It had weathered the storm well and only held a little water. But the rowboat was gone.

The ceremony was elaborate, beautiful. It was held by a small lake. The guests arrived in small painted boats that were rowed by servants dressed in colorful clothing with painted faces. Slowly everyone gathered at the far end of the lake near a waterfall with a carved wooden bridge spanning the pool below it. Many of the guests wore wooden shoes that clattered as they walked on the bridge.

Tables had been set up in a small meadow at the edge of the pool. The morning had melted away, and the sun began peeking between the clouds. A soft light flashed from time to time from the huge glasses on the table. Each one contained a rare variety of goldfish.

Ara felt a little stunned by all the elegance and wealth of the scene, but a growing excitement gradually took hold of her. She glanced quickly at the two other young women who had been asked to attend just as she had. They seemed unbelievably beautiful, but she felt more and more confident, nevertheless, that she would be chosen, without knowing why.

Finally four servants carried a large enclosed divan over the bridge and set it down by the pool. They directed the three young women to kneel at the water's edge beside it. Ara waited for the husband-to-be to step out and choose his bride, but a hushed silence stretched longer and longer.

Finally a black swan appeared, gliding out of the silence towards them, and suddenly Ara understood. It seemed to take forever for the swan to approach as it looked around at the guests and stopped to gobble water-lilies. The angle of the sun on the water seemed to give the dark bird's feathers a blue sheen. Ara's excitement and confidence continued to grow.

But the silence hung suspended in the air as the swan continued to wander aimlessly across the pond, eating water lilies. Finally it swam towards the shore in front of the three young girls. Ara could not resist a quick glance as it passed before her. It was just enough to startle the bird. It waddled ashore before one of the other girls. The girl began running about and hugging everyone.

An old man stepped out of the divan and hobbled slowly to the chosen girl. Ara was stricken with a mixture of relief and surprise as the old man approached. He was very large and leaned to one side as he moved. There was something haunting in the lines in his face as he escorted the girl back to the divan. Ara could not decide if what she was feeling was disappointment or confused relief.

When Ara arrived at Blue's with a fresh loaf of bread, the sun had just begun to peek out again over the quiet sea that seemed to stretch forever into the distance after the passing of the storm. She felt anxious, full of anticipation following what she now felt strongly to be the good news of not being chosen by the black swan.

But there was no answer to her knock. She opened the door. A huge mass of emotions swept over her, ponderous and confusing as if the hut had been filled with them, and now they were trying to drown her. The old man's things lay scattered about the floor, covered in mud that glistened in the morning sunlight flooding in through the windows and the gaps in the slats of wood that had softened and spread apart because of the water and the wind of the recent storm. She looked around the room for something she could not name. She knew the old man had to be dead, and she was struggling through the tremendous sucking mire of her sadness. She knew it was not what the old man would have wanted her to feel at the news of his death. She fought to find her way to emotions that he would have found more acceptable.

She stepped into the hut and her foot slipped on the mud. The hut seemed so empty. She felt as if the air itself had turned to a heavy liquid. It was nearly all she could do to continue breathing it. She moved slowly around the room, touching the old man's things, as if perhaps he were hiding inside one of them and by touching it she could release him.

She turned back to the door and shut it, enclosing herself in the atmosphere of her thick swelling emotions, and there, hanging on the back of the door, was the black silk kimono that she had seen in her dream. As she stood there staring at it, she concentrated on the gold cranes that were poised in flight, sewn onto it in minute detail.

Finally she took it down and stripped herself of her clothing to feel its silk against her skin.

She stood there with the robe on, letting her thoughts of the old man tumble around inside her. She did not know how long she had been standing there when she heard the sound of someone's labored breathing as he climbed the path to the hut. She knew it was not, could not be, the old man. The turmoil of her emotions had finally begun to settle, yet she had no desire to move. She waited. Perhaps whoever it was would pass by.

When the door opened, she struggled up from the bottom of the ocean to say, finally, "I'm tired," but she did not return to sleep, and the door did not close.

THE CONSEQUENCES OF COLOR

A RED DOG barks at the ocean where the man on the balcony of the red house on the cliff collects red pebbles. The dark road passes by the house. Fortunately, it is seldom used.

A large cactus on the balcony of the red house, where the man is quietly sorting red pebbles, flowers only twice in a lifetime. The flowers are red. Eventually another storm passes, and the wind begins collecting red leaves. Soon it has enough and, dusting the dark road, it leaves.

The red dog sniffs at the body of the man who has fallen from the balcony of the red house. There isn't any blood. Eventually he too wanders off into the growing shadows, a small cloud in the distance, drifting like a seed.

MEXICO'S GREATEST POET

PELAYO WAS NOT normally a gray person, but Don Carlos had warned him that it would be best to be that way if he ever expected to pass the test. Don Carlos, on the other hand, was nearly always a gray person, but he had read many articles about poetry and would sometimes even quote some, so Pelayo trusted him.

And that was why today Pelayo was a gray person, walking in his father's gray suit along a dusty gray street on his way to the barn to take the test. It was not a real test, but one that Don Carlos had made up to help get Pelayo ready for the one that he would take later, when he wouldn't even know he was taking a test.

Once when Don Carlos was much younger, (now even his beard and his hair are almost as gray as his barn) he had gone to a large gray building in the capital city, and he had told some people there that he wanted to be a poet, and they had given him some forms to fill out, and he had not known all the answers, so he had never gone back to find out what they would say about his application.

Still, Don Carlos fancied he knew a bit about poetry, and so, when Pelayo had confided that he wanted to become a poet, Don Carlos began helping him prepare. And not the least difficult task in all of this preparation was the test Don Carlos had prepared, which Pelayo would have to pass before Don Carlos would give his approval of Pelayo's new occupation. All the while Don Carlos was helping Pelayo to prepare for his life as a poet, he was also working on the test. The results would be Pelayo's first success, so young to be more already than an apprentice poet.

And so now, two years after announcing his intentions, with many books in his head and many careful observations on all that lived around him quivering anxiously within and a vocabulary nearly as big as Don Carlos', and with a modest understanding of the amenities of dress and ambassadorial good will, (for Don Carlos had explained that since poetry was not a totally supportive means of living in the practical world, it would be best to accept the position of ambassador to whatever foreign country was most anxious to have him), and with all this study and preparation to inform and nurture his natural talents and sensitivities, Pelayo opened the barn door and sat down on the stool in front of the polished board, which Don Carlos had placed carefully over the feed bin in the stall next to Bessie, his only cow, who had come all the way from New England with a very rich and very crazy old woman. The old woman had died not two miles from this very spot, leaving Bessie wandering in the heat with nothing but a plastic nametag to tell her story until Don Carlos had kindly taken her in. Much later it was discovered that Pedro Cortinez had smashed the old woman's car into the fountain in the village. He was flung from the car to the steps of the tavern, and the first to come upon the scene thought he had simply passed out drunk right there on the steps. Pedro couldn't seem to remember anything to the contrary.

The old woman had not died in the accident as some thought, but soon after, of a heart attack. Perhaps the close call and Pedro's condition had frightened her to death. Relatives soon came to claim the old woman's stiffened pale body, but no one ever claimed Bessie. And as she was still giving milk, and Pedro Cortinez had no great desire to explain where the new trailer that he used as a goat stall had come from, and no one had asked about that either, Don Carlos became Bessie's Godfather and Bessie kept right on producing fine milk. And so it came about that Bessie became Don Carlos' second closest friend.

When Pelayo sat down in front of the polished board, Bessie mooed and tossed her floppy head over the top of the stall like a feedbag and let it hang there undisturbed. Don Carlos warned her not to give Pelayo any clues. Don Carlos wrote the test on the board, handed Pelayo a pencil, grasped his shoulder reassuringly, and went off to find a milk pail. Pelayo twisted his head to the side in order to take advantage of the brighter light, which was streaming through a large crack in the side of the barn. Bessie twisted her head to the side too, but for a more pressing purpose; an annoying horsefly had landed on her nose and needed the coaxing swish of her tail to encourage a search for a more congenial resting place. Pelayo read the questions slowly.

1. Why do you want to be a poet?
2. Did you answer question number one completely?
If so please explain.
3. How old are you?
4. Are you now or have you ever been an outsider?
5. Did you feel it was necessary to answer question number four?
6. Does anyone consider you crazy?
If not please explain.
7. Have you ever commited suicide?
8. How old are you?
9. Do you believe in miracles?
10. Did you answer question number nine in less than your lifetime?
11. Do you know what love is?
12. Did you answer question number eleven in less than your lifetime?
13. How old are you now?
14. How many answers did you have for questions number one through fourteen?
15. How many do you have now?
16. If you answer the rest of the questions, how many will you have?

Pelayo looked away from the questions and listened while Don Carlos squirted Bessie's milk against the sides of the metal pail. He could see it was going to be a very long test, and he didn't want to miss any of it. Don Carlos squirted the black and white cat with a stream of Bessie's milk and it sat down to lick itself. Pelayo had seen Don Carlos do this hundreds of times, but today he felt that nothing else in his life had ever been more valuable, and his life wouldn't be complete until he could give this to someone. He forgot all about the test.

AND MOVED QUIETLY ˙

ONCE THERE WAS a happy man who had a son. The son said, "The truth cannot be stated." The happy father replied, "But it can be created."

Just this way the son arrived at the corner of Knowledge and Ignorance, over there, near where the moon bathes, and moved quietly from a moment of pain to a moment of pain.

Meanwhile another plague was raging. An angel was polishing his shoes. There were no other children around to investigate his silence.

The son, predictably, disappeared, and in his place a young boy, fatherless, beat his wet new wings. His sunglasses hid his expression. His eyes had decided to offer something oddly intangible. His feet were tapping restlessly at the father's sudden absence, an insistence that sounded like tarpaper.

Was it the sound of the moon splashing in the street that brought the father back? We'll never know, but the son suddenly reappeared in his father's arms, his shiny little shoes pooling the sky as they shuffled into the laden street, his illness leading him on.

And he danced with his father, holding on to his future wings, as if they wouldn't be needed.

PRELUDE TO A DETECTIVE STORY

A MAN STARES at a camera. He waits for the camera, which stands in the middle of the sidewalk on a tripod, to take his picture. He does not appear to understand that the camera is not facing him, and that even if it were, there would have to be someone behind it to trigger the shutter.

A child is on television. The child is any child. The bed is any bed. But the lovers are not watching the television. Or the bed, which is falling away. Or the bodies, which are no longer theirs. They are watching themselves come true. They are watching two people, who are watching them, and for a while neither couple is unhappy with the other. And the child? The child is on television. The child is not watching itself come true. We do not know if the child will ever come true.

At the left in the dressing table mirror is a framed portrait of a delicate young woman with blond, curly hair, wearing lace and a velvet jacket. At the foot of the bed lies a ragged, brown and white cat. The white paint on the iron bed frame is peeling. Only a foot from the cat is the door. The latch is broken and hangs loose about three inches below and to the right of a large eye chart tacked to the back of the door. A pair of men's undershorts hang from a wooden dowel beneath two small cabinet doors, which are not fastened, but neither are they open far enough to see if there is anything inside. Underneath the shorts is a small sink with chipped enamel and a water-spotted drinking glass. By morning three people will have passed the room and in passing glanced in at the body sprawled on the floor by the bed. They will assume, perhaps because of the cat or the smell of liquor, that the man is not dead. They will be wrong. Later, the police will assume that because the room, the shoes, and the overcoat belong to Thomas Chandler that the body too, is his. They will be right, but who is Thomas Chandler?

A man sits on the side of a bed. He talks to a woman. He tells her he must go away for a while, but he will come back. He tells her that he loves her very much. The woman assures the man that she will be all right. She kisses him tenderly. The man leaves.

Now the woman is sad. She is dressed in a rumpled nightdress. She sits on the worn bed-sheets and gazes into a room, which is empty. She has lived most of her life in that room. Pain for the woman. Sorrow.

Thomas Chandler steps into the bank and walks quickly to the nearest teller's cage. He quietly removes a gun from the pocket of his black raincoat and points it at the teller. Both men remain calm. After it is all over the teller will remove his wire-rim glasses and clean them very carefully before pressing the button under the counter.

The car is from Nebraska where, according to the license plate, only five hundred and twenty other cars were licensed before this one in 1934. The car is black and old and the cab is very square and out of the square window at the back a man is gazing. But the car is not moving. Something is moving. Perhaps it is the man's life.

On the table there are three travel brochures, an empty peanut butter jar, an open newspaper, and a butter knife. Except for these things, the room is extremely neat and orderly. The teller returns from the drugstore with a small bottle of white powder. He removes the bottle from the pocket of his trousers and examines the contents carefully before returning to the travel brochures.

Thomas Chandler steps off the bus carrying a briefcase. He walks slowly, gazing into the shop windows and eyeing the people in the street. From time to time he raises the briefcase to his chest and carries it there as if something very comforting were inside.

The teller pays the cab driver and begins walking quickly in the direction the cab has just come from. The cab driver smiles at the tip, shakes his head, and pulls away from the curb. Three blocks away the teller hails another cab and hunches into the back seat. While the cab moves through the city, he repeats to himself the name of a hotel and a room number. From time to time, as the cab stops for a light, he turns and gazes nervously out the back window. At the seventh light he motions to the cab driver to pull over and again walks quickly in the direction the cab has just come from. Three blocks away he turns to the right and continues walking. The glass exterior of the small vial of white powder nestled in the palm of his right hand inside his coat pocket grows slippery with sweat.

The woman does not cry. She puts the telegram in the garbage and stands quietly staring into the empty room. She lies down on the bed and watches the ceiling.

In the woman's dream the teller is at the door. He is handsome and very well dressed and carries a briefcase. He never opens the briefcase, but the woman knows it is full of money. He comes inside when she opens the door and goes into the empty room. He tells her how he wants her to please him, and she doesn't remember the reasons for refusing him. And then she does more than the teller wanted her to do, and the teller calls her a whore and a slut and makes her do everything he can think of. And the woman thinks she is free now, but in the morning, when the teller reaches for the door, he will turn and wait to see if she is coming with him. And she turns too, looks again at the empty room, puts the palm of her hand against her forehead, and wakes, staring up at the ceiling.

The child is any child, but now something has happened to the child. Has the child been born or has it died? Who are the child's parents? Why don't they pay the ransom? How long does the child have to wait to cross the busy street with the broken stoplight? Who is in charge of the investigation, and why doesn't he have any children? Why does the child seem to be getting smaller? How old is the woman who loved the criminal and why did she refuse to read the newspaper?

The detective presses the black button and waits for the fluorescent light to flicker on. He thinks of the mystery novel lying open on the nightstand next to his bed. He goes over the clues and imagines himself conversing in Spanish with the local people. The butcher slides a large block of wood over the surface of the chopping block and continues slicing meat as the red liquid curls out from the gristle and fat and trickles towards the drain set into the wooden floor. Outside it is raining and a man in a black raincoat stands in the red mud at the bottom of the hill.

In the photograph a man is dead. The photographer moves the photograph into the light and takes a picture of the photograph. Now the dead man is farther away. Now the photographer's neighbor is hammering a nail into the wall.

Now the dead man is lying on top of himself in the photograph. Now the photographer's refrigerator is rumbling softly. Now it is quiet and darkness filters the lights at the window.

IF HE'S LUCKY SHE WON'T NOTICE

HE WAS SITTING alone in his room, feeling miserable and confused, when he realized he wasn't alone. Seven exact duplicates of himself were each doing something different in the room. One was trying to stab himself with a rubber knife. Another was staring at the ceiling and rubbing his crotch. Another was lying on the floor, crying. Another was rubbing the wall with his cheek as if he were trying to get it to respond. Another was feeling the doorknob very carefully as if he were trying to memorize the feel of it. Another was peeking out of the closet. Still another was going from one to the other and staring as if he were trying to figure out what was going on.

Finally he said, "This is depressing," and they all stopped what they were doing and looked at him. It confused him, and he couldn't go on. He had wanted to say, "She's not worth it," but he couldn't.

The phone rang, and one of the duplicates answered it. It was a woman's voice. The duplicate left the room. The others went on with what they were doing until he fell asleep.

The duplicate that had answered the phone came back with an attractive woman who was acting affectionate, but there wasn't enough room left in the bed. While she was looking the other way, he put his heart on the nightstand next to his watch and covered it with the lace runner from the dresser. Maybe with the lights out . . .

His heart glowed. Her tiny feet wiggled like mice beneath the sheets.

It was still dark when he woke. A mouse scurried across the empty closet.

He had an impulse to shake her hand. She was asleep so he did.

WARM AND CLEAR, THE NIGHT

1. CONSTELLATION ALBERT

The name his mother gave him formed the only fixed position in a passing sky, the connecting points given but the boundaries between merely suggested.

A rope of sleep, the silence in the anticipation of knowledge, and the oars of impatient delight; of these his transient universe was constructed.

It's an experiment. It's possible. It's Albert intentional. It's an Albert trajectory. It's an Albert social. It's the median Albert plucked bursting.

And it's a cluster of Alberts; Alberts clumsily daybreaking and night-time Alberts pinned to the firmament. Mapped. A pattern created by the confluence of smaller patterns. Oh who shall discover the mistake? Sudden Albert removed from the unreliable heavens and replaced by more perfect not-Albert stars? Sun-glassed and sun-creamed Albert dismissed from the crowded beach of possibilities?

And still no explanation for the alternative path of his sleeping mind, the mind descended from drifting clouds, the mind you can't touch, the part that can't last.

Then Albert visible in the fat languid last of August. Because Albert's assumed body appears for a while to be Albert. Because in our bodies we must contain our ideas. Because the earth turns more than one direction, all at once, just like our bodies. Because the future is presently a theory. Because every trajectory, celestial or earthbound, reaches farther than its creator.

2. A First Promise

Like this:

There is only one shadow, very large and very intricate.

But not like this:

Horses they had. And pigs. Attics and closets. No place to keep great hearty moans. And no way to separate the pleasure from the pain.

Like this:

The taste of him lingers, her thoughts playing with it, trying to place it into one of the categories of desire.
It's new so it won't fit.
She wants to try again.
The shadow is warm and does not threaten her.

But not like this:

Tiny boxes full of restless anticipation.

Perhaps like this:

No one who knows them is listening and inside was another man named Albert who spoke softly and gestured wildly with his thumbs, indicating either

the way to heaven or a severe disturbance somewhere between impulse and
delivery.

Albert drew a map of the decent portion of an orange. As his author, I
offered to carry his tiny shovel.

3. *Subplot to Authorial Intrusion*

Albert's acceptance of antique individualism had gone bad. That's not all
there is to it, no. I was planning (inserted rebellious Albert) to go hiking off
the coast of Nantucket. But Albert glued his thumb and forefinger together
to indicate his separation from the mysterious absence he had perceived in his
universe as a result of his sarcastic suggestion, and I laughed at myself because
I felt foolish, not because I had considered doing anything I might later regret.

4. *Albert Aflutter*

Nor was Albert digressed, unrelented, or merely expected to fail. Albert
was available. Albert was immediate.

And so it came as a true surprise when false Alberts began appearing nearly
everywhere. Counterfeit Alberts escalating. Incorrect Alberts blossoming.
Deceptively ordinary in disguise, they are being given opportunities.

Alberts pollinating.

And following thereupon: Albert errors. General discontent with Albert
and Albert and Albert. An Albert avoidance explosion. Warnings everywhere.
"Do not mistake these imitations for the real thing." Albert test kits offered at
a discount. Pseudo-Alberts already admitting their failures as you meet them.
Albert failures advertising for other Albert failures. Whole families of future
Albert failures. Illegitimate Alberts deeply astir.

Original Albert listening, paying attention.
A clue without a witness.

Alberts unraveling.

O Albert, what stained and misplaced window of perception has horizoned
the ocean you've become?

Albert restless. Albert outside. Albert not Albert.
And in this way more Albert-like.

Briefly, that portion of the sun that is earthbound visits Albert, leaves a
stain. Albert wavers, interrupts his progress, if progress it was. Sheds Albert.
Still Albert.

Most humans, Albert discovers, are progressive, which Albert understands
to mean "false."
Albert grows definite. Becomes contained. Albert is Albert.
Albert a taste of, not a meal.
Albert sifting the contents.

Albert's clothing encouraged to drift. All Albert ablaze with
uncommunicated essence. Albert lights the grand hall of his future life, shared
now, so soon, with . . .

her.

And she finds the Albert she wants surrounded by less desirable Alberts.
Skilled she must become, at paring away the Alberts.

5. *Unselected Alberts, Lurking*

Unlike Albert the Essence, other Alberts are never absent of Albert. Alberts
unabashedly, relentlessly and merely Albert-like. Alberts illuminated with
further Albert. Alberts composed of only Albert light. Which, it must be said,
fails us. Albert, sweet Albert the Unmolded Childman, carousing deliciously in
soap-drenched bathtub adventures. Adolescent Albert advancing. Young Albert
dockside in the bathtub with a not-yet-fully-comprehended representative of
the confusing childhood of Albert innocence. Could "She" really be just the
neighbor girl playing with Albert toys?

Soon, Albert confessing his imagination's voyages. And soon as well, Albert seeking farther unrepentent voyages. Witness anticipatory Albert, dancing on the tousled bed in his flannel trapdoor pajamas. And yet on the outside, in the public eye, coming-of-age Alberts in cufflinks. Alberts in first lust and Alberts newly, tentatively cultured. Alberts at the billiards table. Alberts choosing the correct fork. Alberts spit-shining the new Albert lustbus.

An Albert reclining. Another Albert smoking. Experimental Alberts unrepentant. Alberts devolved.

More than a few Alberts wrong and a whole bundle of Alberts simply waiting.

6. An Albert Flashback with Recurring Thematic Content

The chicken appears substantially taller than Cowboy Albert, if "tall" applies to a large gawky chicken consisting mostly of legs. Cowboy Albert models a horse-bedecked flannel shirt, soft and loose-fitting, like pajamas, a shirt which may even be pajamas, because the cowboy is still a boy. Lassoes and spurs and yellow horses that are probably supposed to be golden like Trigger are dancing and rearing back all over the boy's chest as he approaches the strangely subdued giant chicken, which is wearing a saddle and a bridle and is not necessarily filled with respect for the heroic man Cowboy Albert has quickly become and perhaps is not ready to follow the boy's commands and chase down the obvious villains or come galloping at the boy's whistle when a narrow escape becomes imminent.

In the next scene, the boy's unreliable memory enters, in the middle of the scene, after the action has taken over from the beautiful and evocative landscape and before the establishment of the hero's soft spot for underprivileged older women (who are not old, but merely older, and strikingly endowed with innocent farm-girl-come-to-town eagerness), large hairy big-eyed dogs and horses with a streak of independence, horses which have not been "broken" but merely "restrained" for the introduction of a worthy companion, who knows when to ride hard and when to rest.

The bank has just been robbed, and the dark double wooden doors spring open. Just as the boy rides up on his giant chicken, the robbers begin pouring

from the bank, themselves chickens, fluffy and small, baby chicken after
baby chicken after baby chicken, running in every direction as baby chickens
do, currency spilling from their beaks as they stop, jerky and distraught,
for a piece of gravel that looks like corn, before pecking the bills back up
again. Again and again they turn and dart quickly in the opposite direction,
pecking and picking.

The boy hero reaches for his gun, ignoring the fluttering clusters of escaped
currency, and the side of the gun falls open, revealing a roll of caps. The hero
dismounts the giant chicken and begins chasing the bank robbers on foot,
discharging his cap-gun ineffectively and then throwing his cap-gun at the
escaping baby chickens, picking it up and throwing it again, and shouting,
"Bang. Bang. Bang." The chickens are too fast, too erratic, too unpredictable,
but the boy hero does not stop trying.

Even before the dream has ended, another dream has begun.

And again, action is required of the hero. Get his sister away from the bank
table, yes, that's what he must do because he understands that the table is going
to explode. He knows that he can do this, but he also knows how hard it is to get
sisters to believe they are ever in any real danger because there have been many
previous narrow escapes and sisters have not learned anything from them.

If the boy hero is not in time, he will have to live with the results for the
rest of his life. Then again, if he is in time, he will have to live with the results
for the rest of his life. He does not even suspect how clearly he will remember
the moment before the table does or does not explode, he cannot remember
which, though the results will be everlasting.

Something very very bad must be lurking there because lurking is characteristic
of the behavior of very very bad things. It's a mode in which they are stored for later
use or are remembered as a kind of indulgence. It doesn't matter what's normal.
Normal isn't going to save anyone.

It's like a chain-link fence without the links. Or the chain.

The boy hero didn't really find any of this disturbing but felt he should
attempt to explain himself anyway. As if he were on trial for allowing himself
to be on trial.

7. Tentative Embodiment of the Love Fixation

Too many lamb's tails were shaking in the distance. Back from the past, his innocence unredeemed. A long time away.

He seemed to be flashing a reader-board across his ample green adult-like sports jacket with the flexed pseudo-confident hunker he had attached to his upper torso. No one even skimmed it.

Out of nowhere, of course, she just appeared. Hair so big it had to be blonde. Any bigger it would have to be red.

What the hell's wrong with you? Hair wants to ask him.

He wants to know that too, but you already know it's not the same wrong he means. Not the same wrong at all.

Certainly he wasn't ready, wasn't ready for her at all, but he found something available in his need.

And she was surprised by him. Offered him one of the river's tender blades. Offered the fog.

Both cut him deeply.

He hadn't given enough away yet to know what he was taking.

And that moment was lying there, chitinous, transparent and frail, an abandoned carapace of sluffed pretensions.

The sleep of accidents. Two spikes of imaginary jade protruding from its nostrils like tusks.

Their words danced, they did, like gyrating couples at the home for wayward children locked in adult bodies.

Her underwear was already pinned to the dart-board.

He couldn't understand the meaning of "avocado lips" in the profile.

He wanted to make her happy.

He was crude end sensitive and hers for the asking. Hers for a caress. Damp and warm and recent.

8. Concerning the Nature of Albert's Tentative Maturity

A nervous jubilance it was. Swollen fire-babies. Great beasts of them.
A fleshy presence dripping like a pleasurable wound. Elevated, nocturnal.

Intellectuals with fat hands tried to understand it. Highbrows with very
low brows. Condensed like the movie version.

And so the observers sat in the boat cracking nuts, populating the lily
pads with little half-shells and describing ovals in the dense air the size of the
beautiful monster they were trying to attract.
Smiles to pollinate an army.
That sloppy encampment was terrible, a real floppy bone, but not guilty
of him.

There are two things we know not about Albert. One of them is how much
there is to know about him and the other tends to wander off alone.

Don't. Just don't. (He was merely holding his spherical interpretation of her
wingéd beauty for himself. He wasn't about to die like somebody's goddamn
fucking eternal flame.)

It appeared, therefore, that he was offering a tiny lace flower that looked
like it had been spattered with tooth enamel. The only guest appeared to be
The Dangerous and Deceptive Moral Lesson, but it was difficult to see past his
green bunny shorts.

We can never be simply ourselves, but if we try hard enough, we can
be ourselves, simply. The bunny shorts refused to quit complicating the
temporary closure.

9. Anticipations of Albert

Albert refreshingly befuddled. Albert open and Albert hungry. Albert
relentless.

Heaven's udders aching with Alberts. Departed.

Inside one envelope, another. You didn't get the prize, but you have to give the envelope back anyway.

The unwitting surrender of a slowly raised curtain.

10. Unsubstantiated Sightings of Departing Alberts

Someone is downstairs and Albert doesn't want to meet him. Albert's parents are gone. He has no brothers or sisters. His friends are home alone where they belong. Albert is home alone, and Albert does not want to meet Albert. How long will it be before Albert knows if Albert is sleeping?

Every time Albert puts his hand into a glove, he wonders if he might not pull off the glove and find nothing there.

Of course Albert hears the voices.

The odor of pineapple and urine. Hung in the air as if you could see it.

Three lizards clutched to the afternoon warmth of the red clay tennis court.

A reddening row of thorn scars where Albert searches in the deep brush, tracking the transgressions of blackberry snipers in glossy feathers who release dark excretions from the mossy limbs of the ancient sprawling oak where they perch, the sweet fruit plucked from thorny veins of thickly proliferating vines covered with ripening berries, harvested in their clacking black beaks, thrown back into throats like so many shots of a dark absinthe, rumbling along the narrow path down bird intestines to the now purple anus, squirting the juice-bloody gel warmly down from above as the birds take flight over intruder Albert, staining deeply, falling on him from the innocent sky.

As if everything were taking place underneath a great weight.

11. Albert Suspended

The Albert heart's sweet pepper fire, the lungs' collections of salty tides. If only we could stop now.

A different note from every stone.

The almonds lined up on the wooden table begin to whisper, one after another. They think Albert is sleeping. They rise and fall and rise again while Albert listens. They shine past the dust-laden stream of window light Albert has failed to adequately surrender to, at once purposeful and hesitant, falling through his skin.

12. Further Embodiments of the Love Fixation

A barely surrounded spilling exuberance of intention.
A fat sack of that.
A nearly tuberous cataract spreading out to squander the generosity of nervous sparrows.

A lost river, a misplaced lake or two.

The iceblue fjords of Albert thought.

The lifting waterchurch of Albert eyes.

13. Albert In the Museum of Morning till Night

I've written you frequently, my letters, like nature, secretly formed and slow to complete their character. Sadly, it's our ideas, not our bodies, that have been hung out like meat.

Snow like silence in a dream. It waits for you.
Snow coming down so softly it goes up and then rests a moment before

deciding to breathe again and continue the journey.

Says Albert unaware of his own transportation.

14. *The Love Fixation Further Defined by Natural Elements*

Pinholes in their skin like the bites of stars.

The almond moons of her deep territorial eyes.

Bobble me tiggly, sweetmeat.

The aged amber temple bells of the heart's columbine.

Like one more beast breathing soft and foul above their sleep.

The voluptuous soft kick of a sudden rain.

All that green breathing takes the breath away.

15. *Further Authorial Intrusions Disguised as Thematic Development*

Something moving between the remaining evergreens like breath, the
sound of woodwhisper lifting like wings.
Am I the owl or the mouse?

I'm gone.
What does it mean when the darkness doesn't arrive?

It's your caution I recognize, the way it spreads the sound of your steps out
across the broader path, as if to claim more of the journey, a kind of authority
without the aggression.

A list of stars arranged by what need, and you, trembling against the skin of one word and one word.

A shadowlump wrenched from the side of the night.

Fat little cherubim with honey-assed bottoms dragging across the embarrassed horizon.

Bundles of possible Alberts.

16. Some Considerations Concerning Her Departure

As if tiny silver flutes were not failing to hide between the trampled grass blades. As if the mangoes in the guest room were not even watching. As if the hurt, as if the flight, as if the strained play. All leading already away.

As if, making damp eyes for each other, they had begun watering down the tears.

The obvious isn't obvious to her who has barely been here.
Albert seems to have altered the altar.

I ask for your love like a train, but you've stationed me. The whistle's for me, yes, it is. No one's leaving. Smoke scheduled the departure. Says Albert perplexed.

An entire cathedral of need, a forest.

17. Delayed Considerations

Gravity lets Albert down. It hurts big.

It's the story of my head, says Albert, which is full. And of my heart, he wants to say, which is fuller.
Which is not longer. Which once was bigger. Enshrined.

And as the net rises in the roiling water, for a fleeting moment, you can see the moon roll, flop and leap free till once more the water settles, inviting reflection on the reflection that contains all Alberts.

And eats at the surface of its world.

And the thieving moon falling through the river's skylight grabs Albert
heart from its wrapped jewelry box, replaces it and slides silently off the roof
and between the negligent seaweed trees.
How does he know if it's passion or fear that holds him here?

Just as her smile detonates, exploding Nature's indifferent loitering. Albert's
never been able to wait like that. He carries his sorrows in a basket.

18. *Absence Coda*

Towering catalpa, white poplar, mountain peppers and mulberry and
Albert's gullet full of minnows. It's the thing inside, see, that feels like silver
babies darting in and out of the stomach bucket.
Cinnamon-downed breast, chestnut ears.

It's not the mountain but the cloud above that's glass, stained milky and
slipped sideways like some child's gigantic silly grin.
And the only other cloud in the sky seems Italian and rising like bread
before the golden skin of morning's warmth slips a calloused hand beneath the
wide empty throat of the love that is leaving, leavening the act of it, a salt-
breasted mare climbing the swollen sea air.

So blooms the wounded face, human and useless but for the explanation of
lines cutting across the forehead's early aging meadow, a kind of browsing in
which the animals drifting do not settle on any one taste or run, fleet, to the
foot of the mountain we have carried here in our eyes.
Does Albert offer the useless tender of a man's fallen heart, dusting up
the redundant melodrama, which is his life and not his direction? Shall we
not go to him in his solitary cell and release him and sigh with him and
whisper to the angry stretch of river swollen with the continual falling of its
star tears?
Albert begins setting his eyes upon the newly sprouted stalks, his new
thoughts climbing across the riverbottom. He's offered himself a choice, oiled

wooden boards dropped down like ancient panels, screens presented to the emperor before the lapse of powers.

Acknowledge.

Even the hint of absence we seek. The other side of the footprint.

A life in the mountain monastery. Three donkeys and a mule.

It's the kind of madness with a rock in it, a hardness at the core that keeps the swelling focused.

The leaftalk of sunstruck branches.

And it's all here in Albert's potatosack overcoat. Unpublishable thorns pierce the deep themes of his regret. A lapis-winged butterfly pulses phosphorescent wings, delighted with its discoveries. It trembles with anticipation as it clings to a fat marmot's warm turd.

19. *Abandonment of Artifice, a Confession*

Albert once again takes his place in the sky, points of light like moments of understanding, here one evening and gone another.

Rain falling lightly, the boat drifting.

Did you?
Yes.
Go home now, someone's waiting.

O Albert. It's not because I miss you that I sing.

IN THE ABSENCE OF SEEDS

TO HIDE HIS CONFUSION he screams loudly. He wants the neighbors to be misled, believe he's only crazy and not a failure. Better if they look right past him. Better if they think he's worthless than worth something that's been lost. So he makes love to a couple of trees. Not at the same time. He's not impossible, just broken.

It had something to do with insects and mythological representations of monumental grief. It had something to do with water.

My eyes are open and something happens which opens them.

The field is freshly plowed. A young girl sleeps in a furrow. Her brother is afraid to wake her. It had something to do with angels and bees. It had something to do with sorrow and the joy that precedes it.

Life removes his mask to find death, who removes his mask to find life, who removes his mask to find . . .

Half a kernel of corn--where has the deer mouse gone?

It never happened. That's what makes us possible.

SHINGLES, AN OPEN NOTEBOOK

FOR THE LAST few days a woman has been walking by the hole in the street where a man is working. She comes by in the morning just after the man disappears down the hole and in the evening just before he reappears and begins rearranging his yellow defense system. Each time she walks by the hole, she stops for a moment and looks to see what is in there. Always that man is there, waiting, posing for a painting of the noble working man.

Another man sits on the porch of the white house closest to the hole in the street. He props a pen against his cheek and gazes quietly out into the street. Sometimes he writes something in a notebook.

Evening. Faint streaks of pink are beginning to stretch out from the horizon, illuminating the soft bellies of clouds. The air is calm and quiet. People are eating. The woman has come and gone as usual, but the man has not yet climbed up out of his hole.

The man on the porch nods. Every few minutes he jerks, sits up straight, and again stares attentively toward the street. The pink bellies streak and begin to darken.

Morning. Two men drop yellow rubber dunce caps around the hole in the street and set up more yellow railings. They back a large motor mounted on a squat yellow trailer up to the hole. They slide a large yellow tube into the hole and start the motor.

Late afternoon. The dunce caps, the motor and the two men are gone. The yellow railing and an orange lunchbox remain. The man on the porch appears with a glass of lemonade. Leaving his notebook on the porch, he wanders out into the street, carrying the lemonade. He leans on the yellow railing and peers down into the hole. He looks around to see if anyone is watching. He climbs down into the hole.

The woman is early. She gazes into the hole. Someone has stolen the painting. She looks up and notices the empty porch. She walks over to it. She notices the open notebook and begins reading. She sits down. Cloud bellies darken. She leans her head back and closes her eyes.

Morning. The chugging of the yellow motor. More dunce caps. Two men are joking loudly. The woman on the porch murmurs and jerks awake. Leaving the notebook, she walks out into the street. She talks with the two men. She gestures with her hands as she speaks. The two men laugh loudly. She returns to the porch and begins writing in the notebook.

Noon. The two men and the yellow motor are gone. The woman wanders out into the street and gazes into the hole. She looks to see if anyone is watching. She climbs down into the hole.

I put the last shingle in place, climb down off the roof and walk over to the porch. I pick up the notebook and begin searching. I begin rocking back and forth.
Slowly, motion begins in the street. Next door a man climbs onto the roof and begins replacing shingles.

TWO LEAVES IN A WOODEN BOWL

EVENING'S PAW touches down softly. A door leans into its hinges. Some other interior, walls bright, windows and doors carefully framed. You were there once. Fog covered the marsh. Light was escaping. Small fires burned in the dry places.

You were the bridge, with a name grown round and smooth. Curled deep where smell is master, tracks waiting.

You have become a cautious undertaker. I have become a hat with a lowered brim. I was the one who found mirrors, throwing back every twitch and habit. I could turn a hundred different handles and find myself behind each one. Still we have not given up comfort, and the light on the porch reaches far into the forest.

I have need of broken things.

I did not come here to question the wind, but wonder is a sturdy cane.

Dusk on the marsh searches beneath a wing for the smoke of entry. I gather my collection of shadows deepening into the haymow. Sometimes my journey likes sitting in a broken chair on a porch at sunset.

Beneath the screams of seagulls glittering all the ears with bright metal, the evening wind flails pine shadows. A dark flurry of fish slips deeper into unexplained waters. Dust covers the hillside in windy swirls. A lone figure descends, disappearing in the rocks flanking the windy path. Leaning into its eyes, a small salamander moves out on a rock.

And in this scene the grove of aspen silvers the light falling from clouds, falling away into the hills without color because silver is not a color, but a lifetime, and yours is here with the leaves.

Go on. Close the door and turn to the candle sinking slowly into the table. In the house of your body you will find an old friend talking to himself, gazing absently at a leaf.

Twirling it.

Twirling another.

LEDA REDUX

1.

I SHOULD LIKE to report a few observations concerning a recent
uncorroborated if nevertheless independent report, citing a rather curious
event as footnote to a study focused on our belovéd swans' juvenile dietary
habits, which described the unexpected and seemingly spontaneous, perhaps
even somewhat amorous exertions of a single large male, who was tossing great
volumes of dust wildly about with his thoroughly substantial wings over an
apparently self-created, appropriately-sized declivity in the loose dry earth,
which had been trampled by a small and somewhat sedentary domesticated
herd of bison, and conveniently, was only a short walk from the site of this
year's meeting of scholars of a kind who might find such an event of particular
interest. The clear majority of participants in the 13th Annual Conference
on Literary Avianism still believed, prior to this latest, and, let it be said, not
very traditional, observation, that swans, in keeping with the more "romantic"
notion of their literary heritage, most certainly do not, I repeat do not, take
dust baths, an activity reported previously and inconclusively in a mere
handful of speculative and untested reports, and, in any case, said swans
appeared to these unreliable sources to have been engaged in not merely for
pleasure but to discourage the numerous unwelcome members of the smallest

of (and let's have it said, most annoying) insect species, those most generally referred to as "mites" or "midges," from taking up residence in the substantial quantity of the famously warm "down" providing our celebrated bird's protection from the all too frequently harsh and challenging elements of its chosen environment.

Could it really be considered coincidental, then, when a most unwelcome rogue conference attendee, who had renamed herself, albeit legally, Leda, chose suddenly (on a whim, she claimed, as if such decisions were visited by muses) to "bathe," thoroughly and brazenly naked, in the dust of the prairie dog mounds barely beyond the carefully protected "natural state" of the river dissecting the campus of the conference-sponsoring Midwest liberal arts college at which an illustrious collection of critical minds was gathering? And when the most "substantial" of the numerous large swans known to return from southerly migrations to the vicinity of the conference hall (yes, indeed, one of the very reasons it had been chosen for the conference) succumbed to her (let's face it) amorous temptations, (though I would venture to guess that would hardly be a swan's way of referring to the event) the great and surprisingly ungainly beast would thereby be risking the negation of the recently established and almost ritually created barrier of protective dust by exposing himself to questionable, if human, fluids. And yes, certain participants could not refrain from speculating on the dust bath's function in relation to the recently increased need for caution concerning certain sexually transmitted diseases (as if the swan had any way of knowing such social changes had transpired), and despite the great beast's noble literary heritage, these self-same icon-shattering punkscribes claim that the handsome creature risked his very health to ravage the beauty come to share his bath. This has, as one might sadly expect in this modern world of sensationalism and factual liberty, become the favorite of several new topics of heated debate at this year's unexpectedly enlivened conference, and inevitably, of far too many scholarly discourses, including one of highly questionable scholarship, published in an Eastern tabloid, which went into a lengthy description of Leda's "Avian Aspect" as noted by a particularly suspect ornithologist not a member of any of the conference's several sponsoring organizations whose credentials have been unavailable for examination.

Was it merely circumstantial then when two roving and avowedly unaffiliated critics appeared, cameras in hand, at an advantageous point of observation to the, it should be noted, somewhat lengthy, aforesaid event and demanded an in medias res forum to debate the meaning of the particulars of the performance they were witnessing as the swan's amatory performance inspired both curiosity and outrage, or had it all been prearranged as a new criticism participatory theory session by the conference organizers? This question was already under severe and contentious discussion when one of the two "freelance" critics asserted that the swan's bearing was entirely too severe, Leda's cries too throaty, the bird/god's sensitivity inadequate, the arch of Leda's back too pagan, etc. etc. until the critics themselves had become more impassioned than the mating couple was reported to have been, despite the further contention by yet another critical faction that not all of that being witnessed, despite appearances, was fully consensual. The rumor then circulated that Leda the Contemporary had, in truth, quickly complained to the two "objective" critics of "rape," and, other more affiliated critics asserted, had accused the two critics, as well, in an ironically meaningful projection of responsibilities, of the same aforesaid violation, later negotiated within this particular limited academic community to the lesser assertion of "critical coercion." An additional rumor then took currency in several unsavory if sometimes humorous forms that the cygnetium gigantium had been inadequate (too inexperienced perhaps?) to his task and further that Leda had actually appealed "provocatively" to the two participatory critics, who had been entirely too preoccupied with their preparation of footnotes to adequately accommodate her, for at that very moment they had been stunned to hear what witnesses asserted to be a clearly human utterance erupting from the god/bird, which can be reported here in a rare and unanimous critical agreement among the witnesses to have been, "I'm a God, not a porno star." A recanting scholar of the Literary Socialism school later asserted, citing precedence in Aldous Huxley's groundbreaking study of sin-hungry nuns in *The Devils of Loudun*, that there had been a "group auditory hallucination fervor/spontaneous procreative disturbance emanation" and speculated on the influence of the coincidental broadcast on cable television, available in most of the conference participants' rooms the preceding evening, of *The Elephant Man* as well as two movies featuring angels and an unnamed "pornographic" Pay Per View Special Feature, the latter offering having been provided as chargeable to any valid credit card with assured confidentiality. The recanter failed to offer a list of her own viewing on the evening in question and thus might be suspect as to the nature of the balance between research and personal experience involved in applying her speculations.

Were I a poet rather than a scholarly reporter, I might choose this moment to ask in all sincerity, "Did our god then fly clumsily into the blossoming skies of misunderstanding?" Most certainly he disappeared. Without having, perhaps, fulfilled his mythological duties, leaving Leda in the lurch and primed to take up the critical cudgel in self defense, her musk-bathed limbs aflutter with excitement, confusion, and insult entirely too intense for most merely mortal conference attendees.

2.

"What, then, is the true nature of swans?" queried an unwitting conference attendee at the following year's conference, kicking at the dust next to the library's neglected W. B. Yeats Memorial Garden during a break in the now highly charged invitation-only panel discussions and wondering about the questionable statuary, which included sleeping flamingos with their heads either broken off or hidden under their wings, undersized buffalo, oversized prairie dogs, and a single tiny elf, as well as several swans of impossibly varying sizes, one of which may have been a goose, all cast in ordinary gray concrete.

"And what then of the misrepresentation of mankind's noblest symbols?" grandly and insightfully wondered aloud this same naive critic in the garden's John Keats Alcove, which faced the Andrew Lloyd Weber Appreciation Bench, taking advantage of a lull in the panel's proceedings to recklessly unzip his trousers. Whereupon he pissed into the garden's murky pond, sighing mightily.

Meanwhile Leda, returned from the preceding year's events as if from a migration, did indeed dress in a snappy powder blue power suit with matching pumps to restrain her feminine charms during the penultimate session of the conference, where she was scheduled to present a paper on the role of the feminist critic in reshaping the literary canon as an act of universal revolutionary enlightenment.

3.

With the clairvoyance of hindsight we now enter the relative future of our critical inquiry to discover, merely eleven years hence, Leda demonstrating

the pioneering techniques of her newly recognized field of Avian Behavioral
Deviation Study by delivering a carefully researched paper on the regrettable
alterations now extant in the widely recognized (and, let us appropriately
footnote, even more widely imitated) mating season dust-bathing behaviors of
recently domesticated swans. Wild ones are no longer available for comparison
(escapees excluded). Thus the importance of the historical dimension of Leda's
first person account.

The Critics Circle Awards Committee is at this very moment convened to
consider a presentation on swan calls enhanced by a commissioned musical
composition engaging their variety and symbolic potential for the Twenty-fifth
Anniversary Conference on Literary Avianism. This they are scheduling to
follow a newly sanctioned gaggle of feather-robed performance poets, likely to
be attended by an even larger swagger of professional preeners and protesting
verbal slamdancers, which, it is hoped, could be included with photographs in
an annotated critical edition of responses to the now fully recognized Swanist
Society by the conference-sponsoring Oxford University of the Frontier West
Press, to be available in time for brisk sales at the next conference as well as interim
conferences planned to coincide with migratory remembrance ceremonies in
both Fall and Spring on campuses of leading educational cooperatives and public
parks on both coasts, which, it is hoped, can be scheduled to help overcome the
lingering effects of last year's diversity presentation by the original sponsoring
institution's justifiably overlooked Research Committee of Irrelevant Theoretical
Interpretations of Erotic Irish Campfire Hornpipes for Female Impersonators and
Their Shepherds, an underground operatic tour de force already discredited by The
Replacement Research Committee as based upon works not by William Butler
Yeats as purported, but actually derived from the paintings of the late Francis
Bacon Junior, to whom more recent research has shown can be ascribed a series of
literary and artistic forgeries of great skill and misguided potential, and it can now
be said, thanks to exhaustive research, that he, the poser, is categorically unrelated
to either the famous writer or the famous painter, his real father having been a
Czechoslovakian talk show host who spent his later years collecting the works of,
no surprise here, famous forgers and their imitators.

"This, then, is the true nature of critics?" queried our forgotten critic-
turned-heckler from the sparsely inhabited auditorium where the extension
course on the history of contemporary critical movements was quickly
shrinking into its own neglected history.

"And the fate of many a sadly domesticated swan," whispered Leda longingly in answer from the far corner of avian obscurity as she once again abandoned academia for a stint of wistful mooning and dust-bathing near the local murky pond.

4.

And under these circumstances, as an untenured faculty member, it has now fallen to me to organize yet another conference. It is therefore my duty to report that Leda has reluctantly, and I must interject, sadly, agreed to speak with us at next year's conference. She now believes it her responsibility to attempt an illumination of the increasingly ironic series of misrepresentations that led to the current devaluation of Swanism. Leda has requested that we "preconsider" certain questions herewith presented in the charmingly contemporary and irreverent style to which we have now become accustomed to being addressed by Leda through her highly vocal and increasingly organized and militant followers.

1. Has William Butler Yeats ever been presented with an adequate understanding of swan anatomy? Under what circumstances?
2. Is the unidentified narrator of the earliest Leda narrative male or female and with what implicit bias is the narrative thus tarnished?
3. What is the meaning of the contradiction inherent in the human understanding of swanness?
4. Why is marriage an irrelevant concept?
5. Do swan feathers carry disease, knowledge, or millions of tiny godheads?

5.

And with my research into the relevance of preceding events now laid out, it has unexpectedly become my sad responsibility to report to this year's conference that our belovéd guest speaker, Leda, is no longer extant among us. The circumstances remain, as might unfortunately be expected, murky.

It has already been decided that these suspicious events will be the subject of our next conference in the hope that our research might assist the duly appointed authorities in their difficult job of sorting fact from fiction and taking appropriate action. Proposals will be requested from select members in attendance at this conference and independent proposals are invited but may be rejected if deemed inadequately stimulating. The pond is reportedly full of feathers this year, only one of many suspicious circumstances in need of our scholarly efforts, and I'm sorry to report that we can no longer tolerate cross-disciplinary dressing in the field house, which will be the sight of next year's conference if we are successful in procuring a house to put in the field. Thank you for laughing. Levity is not always appreciated among our numbers. Training sessions for the facilitation of humor in academic discourse are in the planning stages as well.

And, yes, sadly, the other rumor entered into current circulation is true as well; the president of procurement is retiring this year, and you will all be expected to procure your own staples for next year's proceedings. However . . .

Dust baths we have. Plenty of dust baths.

And water in the river. Lots of water.

And moons. We have moons.

I must remind you, however, that according to the recent presidential directive, public property is incapable of desiring love, and it should therefore not be loved upon.

We can't all be swans.

6.

Excuse me once more, dear colleagues, for interrupting your belated deliberations, but I have been asked to announce that donations in Leda's honor may be sent any damn place you wish. Leda was everywhere.

I am now required according to the terms of our insurance policy to state that we cannot be responsible for your love. Please do not leave it in offices or classrooms. Neither can we recommend attempting it at home as it has become clear that even mentioning it could indeed make us liable, in a sense participatory, unless such mention be accompanied by the disclaimer which this statement represents.

Leda was a professional, and we believe she has gone to a better place. I am not referring to any religiously-affiliated conceptualization, and so I can make this claim without specific offense. I can also announce with great pleasure that Leda has, during her prolonged absence, been awarded tenure. She will, in this way, be one of us in perpetuity.

Thank you for your attention. I believe our conference meetings now constitute a far better world thanks to our diligent efforts at providing a forum for deconstructive conflict resolution. Thank you for arguing with us. Thank you for dedicating your lives to complexity and uncertainty. We will return them promptly upon retirement. It is, indeed, okay to laugh. I believe Leda would like that. Our research indicates that it would have been Leda's desire as well to provide more appropriate refreshments and we have attempted to honor her preferences. The mosquitoes are delicious and available in several different flavors and sizes. Please indulge freely. We have provided a generous assortment in the cafeteria for your consumption on the premises. More exotic fare remains available by the pond, which has been moved further from the building to facilitate a sense of naturalness, however you might wish to define it.

Water is available.

Lots of water.

And dust.

Dust is available.

A THEFT

RATNER HAD SOMETHING distasteful in his mouth and talking didn't seem to be getting rid of it. He seemed to be saying more when he shut up than when he was talking. I wanted to know if he had any jewelry he wanted to get rid of. I was trying to implant the idea in his mind without saying anything about it. I wanted him to think it was his own idea.

"I don't have anything to live for," Ratner said, and I thought, "but do you have any jewelry?" Instead, I said, "Don't be maudlin. You have just as much to live for now as you've ever had."

"That's the problem," Ratner said. "Now I know how little it's always been."

Ratner got quiet and looked out the window. I guessed he didn't really want me to say anything. Raindrops were sparkling where the sun had come out and found them. Happy little clichés of pleasure. It made me think of the longed for jewelry and I got hopeful.

Finally I said, "You have many things of value in your life and people who care about you." I went over to the window and admired the wealthy raindrops. It surprised me how beautiful they were because it was such an obvious thing, and I forgot about Ratner for a minute. He was watching me look at their wealth, and he seemed to be cheering up. I don't know why I didn't notice it before, but his hair was standing up. He wasn't, but his hair was.

"I wasn't there when my mother died," I said. I don't know why I said it, but it seemed to make him happy. So I said, "My father thought I was a loser. I don't even know when he died." Ratner smiled and got up slowly. He thought about it, then went to the kitchen and started pulling things out of the cupboards. "I'm going to make you a cherry pie," he said. "You need some cheering up."

Ratner sat me down at the kitchen table with a cup of terrible coffee. He was whistling something that sounded like heavy metal, and then it turned into "Somewhere, Over the Rainbow." I told him all about the time my mother washed my mouth out with soap for saying, "Shit." He laughed and said, "Shit, that's entirely extreme." I told him about the time my father beat me, but I couldn't remember what for. I couldn't remember my father beating me for anything.

The pie tasted surprisingly good, so I ate too much of it, and my stomach hurt. Ratner stared at my pale available wrist each time he gave me another piece of pie. I was eating too much pie, and I thought to myself, "I want to go now," but if you cut your losses, they come back scarred. I wanted to make myself do something I could be proud of just a little, so I asked him, "Where'd you learn to make pie like that?" I thought he was going to tell me about his mother. I thought he was going to get happy again and make me feel bad, but he answered, "I didn't learn it. It just happened."

He had his head down, and he seemed to be staring at my still available wrist, where the pale scar was, and this time it didn't make me nervous, and I left my hand there, which was waiting on the table and wanted to touch something. I thought maybe it wanted to touch him, so I asked if maybe he wanted to buy my wristwatch, which was too bright and kind of distracting. It was shining in the fresh light coming in through the kitchen window. Sometimes it sparkled. I thought maybe we could shake hands on the deal. I thought maybe we could touch each other.

THE NEW FRONTIER

AGAIN. HUNK WAS wonky. It had something to do with where we lived. We moved to The New Frontier because of Hunk's job at the shoelace factory. The company is "progressive". It moved to an abandoned suburb. Hunk's '57 DeSoto couldn't handle the long drive, so we moved too. To the abandoned suburb where we live in an abandoned building.

Anyway, I was looking out the window we put in the wall that didn't have any windows before we put one there, and I decided that I really didn't mind living like this. I kind of specialed it out, I mean. Like it was mine. Like it was something I had created instead of just moved into.

Well I was looking out the window, see, and I noticed where several Snookered Nomads had carpentered the wooden railing, and I decided things had a nice feel about them.

Quaint, my mother would call it. But not so rural as some abandoned suburbs. There were a lot of empty apartments, for sure, but there seemed to be no serious lack of odd noises. Entertaining noises, I mean, like what the hell could make that kind of sound noises, not someone's dying or going to kill me if they aren't kind of noises.

So finally on the second day I was standing vacuously at the window, proud as a cloud and drifting, when a stretch plodded by with an animal looking thing clinging to his shoulder like a weasel maybe. The stretch seemed to be feeding the animal thing something. The animal thing rubbed its long thin nose in the man's scraggly beard and another nut or piece of fruit or whatever weasel's eat would magically appear in the corner of the man's mouth, and the weasel would snatch it away and chomp on it, as they say in the cable channel nature flicks, "voraciously".

The stretch stopped in front of the apartment and leaned against the recently textured railing. I surprised myself this time by being decisive and going out to talk to the guy. What the hell, I mean Hunk was on his meat and odding out, and I needed a communications fix. So I spoke to the creature.

"Hey, I couldn't help noticing your weasel."

"She's a ferret. I used to train ferrets for a living."

"Not much call for that now, I suppose."

"Yeah, I'm sorta outa work. Ain't nothin' new, though. I'm used to it."

"I don't mean to sound inhospitable or unwelcome-wagonly, but I can't help wondering what the hell you're doing around here because I don't really understand it myself, what I'm doing here, I mean, but it's okay, really, I kind of like it here now, but shit, well, there just ain't many of us around and sometimes I just talk too much."

"I'm looking for a cheap place to root out. I'm thinking about working up a ventriloquist act with Prudence here. Charlie, Charlie Watts. Friends call me 'Digger' and sometimes I talk too much too, okay?"

"I'm Katrina, Digger, and yeah, I mean let's get along, and I wish I could say it better, and I'm no desperation scene or anything but it's specific. I could understand this, easy."

And again. Next day Hunk was still wonky, and I tried to cool him off. He kept drizzling like an indecisive weather report. I brought him French Vanilla ice cream, and he spilled it on his black leather pants. I couldn't stand it. I went out for cigarettes.

Three hours later I came back, and he was giggling with Digger while Prudence snatched nuts from his crotch.

That night I read a story about a man who had lived so deep in the tropical rainforest that all his books had molded and fallen apart. He had written three novels that had all been devoured by tropical ants. I thought I should feel sad, but I didn't. All I could think about was the ants. I woke up in the middle of the night with my skin tingling. The window was open, and it was raining. I thought I should close it, but I just lay there smelling it and tingling.

Hunk decided to build an aviary. It probably had something to do with Digger and his ferret. I hope this is not a feed-the-ferret aviary. Do ferrets eat birds?

At least Hunk is happy. Like a young boy building his first space ship, hammering and nailing and sawing scraps of wood he salvaged from one of the deserted buildings across the street. He found some chicken wire on the roof with tiny little holes so even the smallest bird could not escape. The wire was probably left over from somebody's pigeon coop, but they got the wrong size holes or something.

I hope this isn't all going to end in another disappointment. Hunk doesn't seem to have noticed that the only bird life we have in this neighborhood is a raven that scavenges from the garbage the neighbors put out. Sometimes I used to try to give it scraps, but there wasn't much left the way Hunk eats, and I stopped when I saw it eating a dead cat or something on old man Doodlerai's windowsill.

There's a hole in the middle of the ceiling where the chicken wire extends out onto the roof because we live on the top floor, and it's kind of pleasant to have light in the room when the sun cracks the clouds. The windows were all on the roof and painted black when we moved in, and Hunk hasn't gotten around to doing anything about it except knocking out a hole in one wall and putting some glass in there on that side.

The plants Hunk planted in the aviary are not doing so well. The leaves yellow and fall off. The birds land on them and then flap furiously when their perch falls off and then they do. Hunk studied up on birds and was so sure he got pairs that it's kind of sad that they're all just sort of going through the motions and not really hatching any eggs except the doves that had a crippled baby and two normal ones. Hunk says they're still too small to tell what sex they are, but to me all doves are females. It's probably sexist and all, but it's strange that even when two male doves are in the same cage by themselves, they act like they're nesting, and one of them builds a nest, and the other coos and struts and brings feathers to line the nest. Then if you put a female in there, they fight. Over her and with her. I guess I wouldn't notice so much except for Charlie, and nobody's fighting over me, which is fine, but Hunk and Charlie are so damned happy lately I just don't believe it. And I just look out the window and watch the birds in the aviary. And they just sit on their make believe eggs like smug little invalids for a while, then just get up and leave it, and one of the other birds comes over, and they peck and peck the make believe egg like it's a special treat or something.

Then some days go by and after a while Hunk sets up his easel in the kitchen by the window with the scratches in it, and he's working on some new drawings. It's like he's a new person, and I'm curious to get to know this guy. Charlie is all the time on the roof or out walking or off somewhere teaching Prudence to talk or something. Hunk's drawings are intricate and detailed and shaded with teeny little lines he calls crosshatching. Hunk believes in teeny little lines. He won't use fat lines. He draws landscapes of our neighborhood.

One night while he is on the roof with his birds, I try to count the lines in one of his drawings. I get to five hundred and sixty-three before I lose track. Hunk won't talk about them. They are dark with incredible detail and a depth made up of hundreds of tiny lines, and they are sad but beautiful. And lost, very lost. And moving. He is in love with miniature emotions, and it's wonderful, and I can't stand it because I can't live there with him. He is lost in accuracy, dragging him down and in. And I am afraid for him and happy for him and worried about him and nearly as lost as he is. Like a mother proud of her son's medal for marksmanship.

Charlie wants to take pictures, but he can't afford a camera, so he found out about this way to take pictures with a camera you build yourself out of cardboard or a box or anything you can tape together to keep the light out until you decide to let it in. He made one out of a box of ferret chow, but every time he tried to take a picture with it, Prudence knocked it over trying to get inside the box and eat the film.

Hunk got interested one night when they were stoned and getting off on weird cameras, and they stole all my sewing needles and poked holes in everything they could think of trying to make lenses for their weird camera ideas. Hunk's thumb swelled up from an infection he got from a dirty needle and Charlie took a picture of it with the iodine box and the penicillin bottle. It looked like his thumb was as big as his head, and I started calling them both pinheads. Charlie went looking for a rubber glove big enough to make cameras in all the fingers, so he could hold it up to make people stop, and then he'd take their pictures while they tried to figure him out.

Charlie just bopped his head around the bedroom door and puckered up his mouth like a silly kiss then ran back in the closet. It weirded me out a little, but I figured maybe he was flirting, so I followed him into the closet. He got mad at me for exposing his film. When he explained that he'd just invented the mouth camera, I laughed, but he was serious. He pissed me off when I tried to take a shower and he kept poking his head in with his lips all puckered and then running to the closet, but finally I got into it and put a mirror in front of his face and called the police about a guy exposing himself in my apartment. Charlie forgot the phone was dead. He looked a little scared. I called his mother and told her her son was exposing himself to strange women. Then I called Hunk at work and told him a pinhead was molesting his wife. Finally Charlie figured out the phone was dead and laughed and exposed himself, this time without a camera. I laughed and made him pose for a multiple exposure. We didn't have to mix any chemicals to develop it.

I'm sorry, but I find it simply disgusting when political prisoners turn out to be animals or deviants, and it's happening all too frequently these days. I don't understand how those Save-the-Whales people keep from getting bored, but at least they don't have to worry about their time and energy, excuse me, but it's how I feel right now buggered away in some low life's . . . well I don't have to say it do I it's just too much it really is . . .

I was dreaming Hunk had a new job at the shoelace factory, and he had to go around to all the employees and make sure all their shoelaces were tied because they were all supposed to set a good example. Only he couldn't interrupt their work or anything, so he had to follow them around all bent over and wait for them to stand still long enough to tie their shoelaces. He got a promotion when he learned how to tie them while they were walking. When I woke up, Prudence was tangled in a ball of twine on the floor. She looked confused, but contented for the moment. I fell back into bed with a soft thump, rolled over and dreamt about my mother's last parking ticket. The policeman's shoelaces were untied.

Charlie bought a station-wagon. I was delighted till I found out he intended to make a camera out of it. He covered the back with black cloth and put a hole in the lift-back keyhole. At least there's still room for all three of us and Prudence in the front and now Charlie takes me for a ride a lot so he can take more pictures.

The finches had babies. They're incredibly tiny and incredibly noisy. It was driving Prudence crazy. Hunk had to find some pieces of glass and put a front on the aviary. Now the birds are quieter, but it's like they're outside again. I got Hunk to make one of the pieces of glass slide, so I could open it when no one else was around to be bothered.

Last night Prudence caught a rat. She was waiting with it at the foot of the bed this morning. Hunk thought it was disgusting. I though it was cute. Tomorrow he leaves for Venezuela for the International Shoelace Convention. He'll be gone two weeks. A lot of shoelaces.

Last night before he packed, Hunk was sluffing. He does that when he has to change. He's a thoughtful man but distant sometimes when that happens. He gets whims in the middle of a quiet moment like a silly kid. It can be wonderful like when sex is great and serious and he gets silly and fun afterwards, or it can be weird. Last night he decided one of Charlie's station wagon photos was a masterpiece. It's huge. He drew a big fireplace on the wall and stapled the photo over it. It was upside down, but Charlie didn't get into it. A picture of all of us having a picnic and skinny-dipping. Prudence sitting in the empty picnic basket watching us. I smiled and went to sleep. In the morning he was gone.

Finally, "Digger and Prudence" feature on the Suburban Amateur Hour, and they win a place in the semi-finals. Isn't that something? Charlie's ecstatic, Prudence is overfed, Hunk is tied up in South American shoelaces and me, I'm just "hopling my dildong" as my brother used to say when Mom caught him staring off into space, wearing his plastic sixguns and battered straw cowboy hat. I loved that phrase. Mom hated it. Charlie thinks it's dumb. I don't know what Hunk thinks anymore. Three weeks of South American shoelaces and only one stupid postcard with a toucan on it: "The weather is here. Wish you were beautiful." Charlie made Prudence tell it as a joke in their act. Have you ever heard a ferret with a Rodney Dangerfield accent?

One afternoon the street is suddenly filled with people. Filled with people in this deserted neighborhood! They are running as if they have been running for a very long time. Their heads sag, and they seem to limp even as they run. Digger fixes a sandwich and takes Prudence outside on the steps to watch. Some of them wave feebly and others ignore them. An hour later the streets are empty again. "Where were they going?" I ask Digger, and Digger says with his mouth full of Braunschweiger, "Home?"

No second booking on the Amateur Hour. Digger thought it went well, but his agent quotes unknown philosophers on the virtues of patience. Digger thought of changing Prudence's name to Patience for new jokes, but it confuses the poor creature. He's considering a commercial for Ferret Chow, but it makes him feel like a has-been. I don't sleep well now. A neighborhood owl frightens the birds in the aviary and the quiet after he passes is almost as loud as the silence of the bedsprings. I need my Hunk.

Dreadlocks on the street with reggae pounding and the neighborhood is happy and filling up, but Digger isn't. He doesn't eat and slaps earmuffs on his head when the fathappy apathetic young whiteguys pretending to be "Jamaicans" gather on the street. Six weeks and nothing new from South America. Are the phony "Jamaicans" working in the shoelace factory, or do they hibernate during the daylight? Nights the neighborhood is jazzed and slick with smiles. Days there ain't enough conversation to tickle a pigeon. Digger's a drag, and I'm heavy bored. Maybe I'll go to Jamaica to get away from the Jamaicans.

Digger's black eye looks mean. He tried to take a picture of a "Rastafarian" with his oatmeal box camera, and the guy thought he wouldn't open the box because he was holding out on his stash. In the photograph a dreadlock ghost drifts like Long John Silver across the plank over the irrigation ditch where the sewer used to be. Digger framed it with a trash bag and old newspapers inside an industrial gasket spatter-painted with ferret dung. A cosmic joke, but Digger doesn't laugh much these days. When the "Jamaican," whose name turned out to be Harvey, saw the picture, he apologized with an oatmeal box full of kickass ganga. Digger and Prudence have been flying, and I'm pissed. I had to get a job at the new groc shop, and they never wait for me to get off. It's funny to hear Digger throwing his voice all over the room and the davenport ragging on the broken lamp and the leftover pizza whining about respect and the sad state of recent olive oil imports. One night the welcome mat propositioned me. I hate it when they party without me. Another night Charlie was asleep on the rug with a torn-open teddy bear beside him. Prudence looked up from the oatmeal box like a kid caught red-handed, teddy bear stuffing clinging to her fur like a snowstorm.

Ha! The police at the door and Digger and Prudence with them. Digger's been mistaken for a lunatic. He lost his ability to throw his voice and started talking to himself on a park bench. A young girl thought he was having a seizure. I show the cops the video tape of the Amateur Hour and they leave. Digger and I argue about our relationship. The glue's gone. I go to sleep and Digger is still arguing with himself, thinking he's throwing his voice, when I wake up to go pee.

Ten weeks and no Hunk. Slippery with deprivation, I stalk the streets. Newspapers on a park bench with feet. Shoelaces untied. I tie them and Hunk screams unfinished in the continental drift of my hungry headheart.

Charlie? Charlie? Charlie, wake up, damn you. I can't sleep. You could talk to me. You could try throwing your voice again. It's a dog moon, Charlie, that ring around it just crawling under your skin like an orderly little herd of ticks. Charlie, wake up, damn you. Charlie?

Slick as a hunk of headcheese and just as clammy. Charlie's got another hangover. Where's Prudence? I ask him again. He's in the shower burbling and slapping the top of his head. I can't take this. Where's Prudence? The hot coffee spills on his hand when he reaches for it. I'll miss her more than I'll miss Charlie.

I go to Woolworth's to buy cracker jacks and to White Drugs to buy cough medicine and to Fuji's five and dime to play with the cheap toys. I buy a little bag of paper drink umbrellas and think about Prudence. I buy candy-striped shoelaces for my sneakers and think about Hunk. I go home and let the birds go. Two of them fly out on the roof and crashland. A crow squawks, and they run back in the cage. I close them in to keep the owl out.

I frightened the birds again, especially the little buggers. The finches were in a panic. One of them got his foot caught in my hair and dangled down my forehead, his wing flailing my eyebrows. I went on a cleaning binge and they perch restless now, hunkered down tired and nervous on the new tree limbs I gave them. The room is spotless. I think I like it, but it feels out of place in this neighborhood.

A postcard from Hunk. No return address. Postmarked Argentina. Seven ducks in surfer shorts raiding a refrigerator. No writing, just my address in Hunk's sprawl.

Three dark-skinned clean-shaven men in business suits and dread-locks walk down the street with a long-haired blonde white man. They're boppin' and cruisin' and rappin' and marchin' and holding their suit coats wrapped tight around machine guns. I want to laugh. I want to go home, but this is home. I want to be bored again. Shoelaces seem so friendly now. I want to be a peasant, overlooked and timeless and as hungry as it takes to live like an animal, an animal with shoelaces and a job that doesn't pay much but keeps you out of trouble.

The postcard looks like the last supper, but a South American military leader sits at the head of the table and smiles. I try to imagine what he would be saying, but all I can see is him smiling and smiling.

I couldn't sleep. Moonlight and the streets glisten with rain. No one is out but me. I peer into the lives of the few people with lights on and windows open to the fresh smell of the cleared air. It's wonderful until I see him. A young guy with his head shaved. No shirt in the cool evening. Khaki shorts and barefoot, cleaning a rifle on the steps of the apartment building across the street from the drugstore. He smiles as I pass.

The next postcard is white, all white. No picture, no writing except the address. White.

I heard them in the streets last night. Like thunder, but I knew right away what it was. Tanks. For weeks the angry homeless exiles and the rest of them I just call the lost have been drifting in and holing up in the other abandoned buildings. I put up an official looking sign I found that warns about quarantine, and they stay away from my building, but I get lonely, and they think I'm diseased.

Maybe it's better this way. I don't know if I could bear their sadness and anger.

The tanks began moving again at dawn, and I sat on the steps by the quarantine sign and watched the people milling about, watching and jiving and pretending not to be scared. A group of young men were acting like kids playing war games, shooting each other and dying and getting up again just as the tanks rolled close to them. One of them set a bunch of red roses on a tank and another one was hunkered down behind the tank in a pea coat like an infantryman clearing a mine field or a young boy sneaking up tiptoe to scare his playmates. He made an odd familiar gesture with his left hand as he plucked a rose from the tank, and I knew it was Hunk. He tossed me the rose without a word and went back to the other young men. I saw one of the men throw something, and as I reached down the steps for the second rose, I heard them open fire and one of the men laughed.

ACKNOWLEDGMENTS

Grateful acknowledgment is due the editors of the following magazines in which some of these works have previously appeared.

Bitter Oleander: "Two Leaves in a Wooden Bowl"
Crosscurrents (California): "Mexico's Greatest Poet"
Crosscurrents (Washington): "Train Song", "A Warm Rain Began to Fall"
CutBank: "Shingles, An Open Notebook"
Eunoia Review: "Leda Redux"
Fine Madness: "Gifts of Silver Fish"
Green Mountains Review: "The Black Swan"
Knock: "The New Frontier"
Mississippi Review: "The Consequences of Color"
Montana Review: "If He's Lucky She Won't Notice"
Northwest Review: "Eye of the Beast"
Permafrost: "Prelude to a Detective Story"
Portland Review: "A Delivery", "Unnatural Attractions"
The Puritan (Canada): Warm and Clear, the Night
Quarterly West: "How I Died in the War"
Santa Monica Review: "Paul Klee's Illegitimate Grandson Considers the
    Evidence Concerning His Deceased Brother's Literary Intentions"

Seattle Arts Image: "A Brief History of Divorce"
Skidrow Penthouse: "Blue Theater Made of Fields and Mirrors"
Sugar Mule: "The Rules of Engagement"
Swallow's Tale Magazine: "A Brief History of Love and Death in the
    Black Forest"
Written Arts: "That Night His Father"
Yarrow: "Near the Church at Cortovino", "Near Torshavn, Faröe Islands"

"Shingles, An Open Notebook" was reprinted in *The Montana Review* in
a special issue of short short fiction titled *Time Enough for the World* and
in the 40th Anniversary Volume of *Cutbank Magazine*.

RICH IVES has received grants and awards from the National Endowment for the Arts, Artist Trust, Seattle Arts Commission and the Coordinating Council of Literary Magazines for his work in poetry, fiction, editing, publishing, translation and photography. His writing has appeared in *Verse, North American Review, Massachusetts Review, Northwest Review, Quarterly West, Iowa Review, Poetry Northwest, Virginia Quarterly Review, Mississippi Review, Dublin Quarterly, Fiction Daily* and many more. He is a winner of the Francis Locke Memorial Poetry Award from Bitter Oleander and the Creative Nonfiction Prize from *Thin Air* magazine. He has been nominated twice for The Best of the Web, three times for The Best of the Net, and five times for the Pushcart Prize. His writing has appeared from eleven different countries. A fiction chapbook, *Sharpen,* is available from The Newer York Press, a book of hybrid forms *Tunneling to the Moon,* with a work for each day of the year from Silenced Press, and a collection of poems, *Light from a Small Brown Bird,* from Bitter Oleander Press. He lives on Camano Island in Puget Sound, north of Seattle, and is also an artist and a musician currently concentrating on dobro and fiddle among the many instruments he plays.

LOS ANGELES

TITLES FROM
WHAT BOOKS PRESS

POETRY

Molly Bendall & Gail Wronsky, *Bling & Fringe (The L.A. Poems)*

Laurie Blauner, *It Looks Worse Than I Am*

Kevin Cantwell, *One of Those Russian Novels*

Ramón García, *Other Countries*

Karen Kevorkian, *Lizard Dream*

Patty Seyburn, *Perfecta*

Judith Taylor, *Sex Libris*

Lynne Thompson, *Start with a Small Guitar*

Gail Wronsky, *So Quick Bright Things*
BILINGUAL, SPANISH TRANSLATED BY ALICIA PARTNOY

ART

Gronk, *A Giant Claw*
BILINGUAL, SPANISH

Chuck Rosenthal, Gail Wronsky & Gronk,
Tomorrow You'll Be One of Us: Sci Fi Poems

PROSE

Rebbecca Brown, *They Become Her*

François Camoin, *April, May, and So On*

A.W. DeAnnuntis, *Master Siger's Dream*

A.W. DeAnnuntis, *The Final Death of Rock and Roll and Other Stories*

A.W. DeAnnuntis, *The Mermaid at the Americana Arms Motel*

Katharine Haake, *The Origin of Stars and Other Stories*

Katharine Haake, *The Time of Quarantine*

Mona Houghton, *Frottage & Even As We Speak: Two Novellas*

Rich Ives, *The Balloon Containing the Water Containing the Narrative Begins Leaking*

Rod Val Moore, *Brittle Star*

Annette Leddy, *Earth Still*

Chuck Rosenthal, *Are We Not There Yet?*
Travels in Nepal, North India, and Bhutan

Chuck Rosenthal, *Coyote O'Donohughe's History of Texas*

Chuck Rosenthal, *West of Eden: A Life in 21st Century Los Angeles*

Chuck Rosenthal & Gail Wronsky, *The Shortest Fairwells are the Best*

What Books Press books may be ordered from:
SPDBOOKS.ORG | ORDERS@SPDBOOKS.ORG | (800) 869 7553 | AMAZON.COM

Visit our website at
WHATBOOKSPRESS.COM

www.ingramcontent.com/pod-product-compliance
Lightning Source LLC
Chambersburg PA
CBHW020619120726
47905CB00003B/859